Polar
PERIL

MARGARET POLLOCK

To Kelley & Guy —
please enjoy!

Margaret Pollock

For all those – children and adults alike – who love polar
bears and recognize them as a sign of
the ecological peril of our polar regions.
And for the Mohawk people, who inspired this story.

CHAPTER ONE

THE STRANGER SAT AS IF she ruled—arms wide, palms flat on her table under the pine trees. She presided over a display of carvings for sale. That part was ordinary. But as twelve-year-old Nikki Brant watched from a distance, she felt the woman gather power into her person. Nikki even felt the pull. The woman seemed mighty enough to preside over the entire Mohawk Indian Strawberry Festival. Nikki wondered if their chief had met the stranger yet. She took a sip of cold strawberry juice and studied the situation over the rim of the cup.

The stranger's table was last in a curving row of Mohawk crafters offering deerskin clothing, wooden flutes, turquoise jewelry, pipes and tobacco, and so much more that Nikki's head spun with colors and shapes and ideas. All morning Nikki visited the crafters. She knew them from strawberry festivals before, and they chatted like family. She liked to help sell, because she was allowed to handle the amazing stuff. She got to wear a tall white-beaded headdress, until a woman in a traditional outfit came by. She was stunning in a long-sleeved smock, straight

1

skirt, and leggings—all of rose red cotton—embellished with black velvet neck and cuff facings. The customer admired the headdress and remarked that it made Nikki's green eyes snap. She tried it on, bought it, then adjusted the headdress on her wavy brown hair and sashayed off with a snap in her own gray eyes.

Now that Nikki had seen all the other crafts, she hung back near the last table and tried to decide if the stranger was good weird or bad weird. She was a big woman, with a wrinkled reddish tan face and hunks of necklaces hanging over a bright print shirt. Then, as Nikki watched, the woman took off her Boston Red Sox cap. White hair puffed down to her waist, but the whole top of her head was shiny-bald. Nikki choked on her juice and backed away step by quick moccasin step.

The woman looked like a witch. Or a spirit woman. Or maybe a seer. Nikki was outta there, but not quickly enough. The woman cast her power over Nikki, and when she said, "Hello, young lady," Nikki couldn't resist. The seer, if that's what she was, reeled her in like a trout.

"Hi," Nikki mumbled. She inched over to the table and would not look up. Nikki sensed she would be helpless if she let the seer look into her eyes. Then the woman could trespass on her thoughts, walk around inside her brain. Nikki's grandpa told her that in the old days everyone was a seer, able to look right into heaven. Everyone could communicate spirit-to-spirit or mind-to-mind, like ESP. But now those abilities were dried up, like a shriveled appendix. These days a seer is rare. Nikki commenced to wad the empty paper cup between her nervous hands.

2

She fixed her sights on the display table. All she allowed herself to see of the woman were her hands. These had delicate tips and fat fingers. Ten large silver rings, each set with a different-colored stone, rode the knuckles. The hands relaxed and Nikki felt the woman's power retreat into her bed-pillow-size bosom.

Now that the force wasn't gusting around her, Nikki decided she could stay for a minute. She examined the display and was captivated by the carvings—some in wood, some in stone, others in bone. Nikki forgot to be scared while she studied an owl, a fish, a Mohawk hunter. She touched a turtle with the tip of her finger.

"Do you like them?" the woman asked. Her voice was sawdusty, like you could sweep it away with a broom. "I was waiting for you to come. I've saved a special carving for you."

The woman dragged a box from under the table and rummaged until she found the carving, which she set on the blue velvet tablecloth. When Nikki laid eyes on it, every other carving on the table receded from view. This carving was beyond all others. Pale wood, it had a polar bear's long back and big feet, bullet head, and shiny black stone eyes. The bear's neck curved so his face looked to one side, like he just heard something over there. Did the seer know Nikki collected polar bears? That she had a bookshelf of photos and stories and science on polar bears, the Arctic, and global warming? That she wished with all her heart she could help the bears survive?

"Can I hold him?" Nikki asked, stealing an upward glance veiled by her eyelashes. The woman nodded. Her skin crinkled

3

at the corners of her blue eyes. She smiled with good teeth. Now she looked kind.

Nikki stood the bear on her palm and lifted him up. He was the size of an egg and weighed hardly anything. She stroked his back, textured with tiny carved marks like fur. She looked at his face. She sensed something magnetic emanating from the bear. It locked her together with him. *Was he looking back at her? Were his eyes alive? Too crazy!*

"There's something creepy about that carving." Nikki threw it down like a rotten fruit. She scrubbed her palm on the skirt of her tan summer dress. The woman stood the bear back up on his feet, head turned toward Nikki this time.

"That bear has a spirit. You can believe me or not, but I tell you, I felt something special as I carved the wood."

"It's a polar bear."

"It is."

"But we only have black bears around here. Why did you choose a polar bear?"

She guffawed at that. "The wood shaped itself as I carved. Seemed like the polar bear was in there and had to get out. Magic, if you ask me."

No matter that Nikki was on guard against the weird, she had to have the polar bear. "How much does he cost?"

"Oh, I'm not selling him."

Nikki stamped her foot. "Then why did you let me get interested? That bear and I have to be together. I must have him."

"Oh, yes, you and the polar bear must be together. But you may not buy him. He's a gift."

"That's not fair, either. Look, I brought money. I can pay you twenty dollars." Nikki fiddled a folded bill out of the deerskin pouch at her waist and smoothed it on the velvet cloth.

"My girl, keep your money. The polar bear is priceless."

"I don't get it. You're just messin' with me, and I don't take that." Nikki turned away, getting madder and madder, face getting hotter and hotter. "I'm sorry I ever met you. You don't belong here. Go away!" Nikki yelled over her shoulder, and jogged out of sight around the corner of the barn. She knew she should be gracious to strangers, but not this one, for sure. Nikki placed the flat of her hand on the splintery red barn wall and stole a look back at the stranger. The woman appeared unperturbed. Nikki's angry words, meant to hurt, had fallen to the ground, like the useless arrows of an inexperienced archer.

"Come back, Nikki, there's more you should know," the woman called. Okay, that got her—the stranger called her by name. She must be a true seer. So there Nikki was again, back at the table with the polar bear.

"How do you know my name?"

"How do you suppose?"

"I think you know the spirits. I think a spirit told you my name." Nikki had never been in the presence of a seer before, and she felt skittish as a fawn. At the same time she was hugely curious.

"Very good. Now listen. This polar bear is meant for you. You know Mother Earth's polar bears are threatened? They might die out."

Nikki nodded. She worried about the polar bears. When Nikki got worried her eyebrows crumpled, which she could feel happening.

"Tell me about them," the seer said.

"I've read a lot about polar bears. These guys are super-adapted to their environment. They're white for camouflage where they live and hunt, on white Arctic sea ice. They eat seals, which are polar bears' perfect food, because seals are blubbery and polar bears need to keep up their own thick layer of fat." Nikki played with the carved polar bear while she spoke, and poked him for fun when she said fat.

"That's right, young one. Tell me more."

"Living on ice floes, polar bears are always in and out of the water. They have webbed feet, their nostrils close under water, and they can swim pretty far. Their scientific name is *Ursus maritimus,* sea bear. I think that's so cool." Nikki looked up at the seer.

"Cool, indeed. Do you understand the danger these creatures are in?"

"The planet is warming and sea ice is melting faster than anyone expected. Arctic ice reflects hot sunlight away from the earth. But when the ice melts, there's less to bounce back the sun, and the planet warms faster." Nikki felt like she was in school, answering the teacher. She didn't expect it at the Strawberry Festival.

"What does melting Arctic ice have to do with polar bears, my girl?"

"Why do you want me to tell you all these things?"

"I must determine if you are prepared for your assignment," the seer said.

My assignment? What assignment? Nikki wondered. Then she answered the seer's question. "What does melting Arctic ice have to do with polar bears? The ice melts and that's the polar bears' world, where they live and hunt. When the sea ice is gone, maybe the polar bears will be, too." Nikki wasn't weirded out anymore. She just felt hollow.

"You've spoken well. Now listen. The polar bears need you. You will learn how to help. This magic polar bear will take you to good places." The woman opened Nikki's hand and placed the bear carving in it. Then she turned away and got busy with something in the back of her booth.

So there Nikki was, wandering around the farm field on which the Strawberry Festival was playing out, holding this amazing carving in her hand. *Spooky carving.* She tucked it into the deerskin pouch and found an empty picnic table under the giant, open-sided tent. She climbed onto a bench and stared across the table into space. She felt rather blank. She thought it was a strange thing for the seer to say, "This magic polar bear will take you to good places." The polar bear was just a toy. Magic? She didn't believe in magic. And how could he take her anywhere? She's the one who would take him. "The polar bears need you?" She knew they're in danger, but what could she do except worry? She's just a kid.

Then who should come galumphing toward her but Charlie-Chum, her cousin and best guy friend. *Excellent.* Same age, same school, same class. And Mohawk, of course.

"Thought I'd find you here," Chum announced. "Brought you some food."

She'd ignored lunchtime and now her stomach was seriously growling. "Chum, you are the best. I'm starving." She inspected the plate. "You got my favorite strawberry cream tart."

"Last piece."

Nikki loaded a forkful. The crust crunched between her teeth like a sugar cookie, a smooth layer of custard slid over her tongue. Juicy berries burst in her mouth. In the first bite she savored each part. But the rest she downed straightaway. Nikki was not a dawdler when it came to good food.

Charlie-Chum took a seat across from Nikki and ploughed into a giant buffalo burger. Ketchup squeezed out when he bit into it, and she shoved a napkin under the drip. *Got it. Of course he had no paper plate. Were all boys like that?* While occupied with food, they shared silence. *Who knows what was in his boy mind?* Nikki was thinking about the carved polar bear and what the seer said.

"So, Charlie-Chum ..."

"So, Nikki ..."

"Wait. I started first."

8

"Come on, Nikki, you'll like this one. See, this guy with two left feet walks into a shoe store."

She sighed. "Yeah?"

"He says, 'Do you have any flip-flips?'"

"Ow, Chum, that hurts," she laughed and smacked her head. His jokes were nuts.

Charlie-Chum laughed too.

Nikki grabbed the sleeve of his deerskin jerkin and shook it for emphasis. "Listen, I gotta tell you what just happened to me at the craft booths. Okay? This is serious."

"Okay, I'm ready. No more jokes. Tell me what's so serious," Chum said, putting on a ridiculous crazy face that cracked her up.

"Stop it, Chum. Pay attention." She shoved his knee under the table, then told the whole story about the seer and the magic polar bear. At first Charlie-Chum was silent. Considering.

"You are some special girl, Nikki," he finally said. "I've never heard the elders tell anything like this." His eyes showed respect. A flicker of excitement, too. "Do you have the polar bear? Can I see him?"

"Sure." Nikki slipped the polar bear out of the pouch and handed it to Charlie-Chum. The carving looked insignificant in his baseball-player hand. Chum had a man-in-the-moon smile on his broad face as he stroked the bear, looked at his eyes, and made the bear walk up his sleeve.

"Where's the seer? I'd like to meet her."

Nikki pivoted and pointed, but the space was empty. The seer and all her stuff were gone.

"She's gone ... but she was there a few minutes ago. I swear."

"No big deal, Nikki. You got a really good polar bear here."

"Thanks."

"But he feels kinda funny. Like he has a magnetic field wrapped around him. My blood's zinging. What's with this thing?"

"I think you're feeling the magic, if there is any."

"You know a sacred spirit can hide itself in anything, living or not? This wooden polar bear could have a spirit. And spirits can do magic."

"You think so?"

Chum nodded and handed the polar bear back. "Besides, a seer made him."

Nikki stuffed the carving into her pouch. Both kids slouched toward each other onto the table, resting their chins on their hands. They were very close. Their foreheads touched. They whispered and no one could hear.

"Charlie-Chum, the seer grilled me about polar bears and the danger of them dying out."

"How cum she did that?"

"Said she was testing to see if I'm ready for my assignment. I'm supposed to save the polar bears. How nuts is that?"

Charlie-Chum sat up. "That is truly nuts. I mean, it would be a great thing to do. But all kinds of scientists and park rangers and people like that are working on it, and I bet even they don't know how to save the polar bears. Don't get me wrong; you can do almost anything. But not save the polar bears. That's not an assignment for you."

"You're a big help!" Nikki sat up, too. "Just for that, I'm going to make you help me do it." Chum laughed. Nikki changed the subject. "Say, I saw you with the medicine woman all morning."

Chum beamed. "Yeah, I'm really into that stuff. She's been teaching me, says I have a gift for traditional medicine. Everything she knows came from her grandpa, and she's handing it down to me. I feel real proud. Today she gave me my own medicine kit. You know what she told me? The Creator made all kinds of medicine, for us and for the bears and birds and every kind of creature, and put them here for the taking. But we forgot about them. Now, if we go to collect any of the medicinal plants, they smile from ear to ear to be of service to us or the animals, 'cause that's why they're here. And I guess the Creator smiles, too, 'cause we remember."

"Chum, that's super! Can I see your kit?"

"It's over with the medicine woman. Come on, I'll show you."

CHAPTER TWO

A DIAGONAL AMBLE ACROSS THE field took them to the medicine woman. "Hi, Grandma. Nikki wants to see my new kit."

"She's not your grandma," Nikki whispered. "Hello, Grandma," she added. The medicine woman, who nodded a greeting then went back to her book, looked plain as mud. Chunky figure, big waist, flabby flesh beneath her chin. Cheap old glasses, the kind you get from the Lions Club. She probably made great cookies. Nothing suggested her healing skill at all.

"Naw, but she acts like a grandma to me, so I call her that." He dragged a lumpy thing from under the table and motioned for Nikki to sit with him in a shady spot. They couldn't help crushing buttercups the wildflowers were so bountiful. Reverently, Charlie-Chum removed the outer covering, a soft old pillowcase, revealing a wooden chest the size of a thick shoebox. He drew a key out of his deerskin pouch and opened the brass lock. He lifted the lid, hinged at the back. Then he pressed a brass button inside and double-layered trays sprang up. Under the lid, colored diagrams and secret stuff were pasted. Nikki whistled in appreciation.

"Chum, this is unbelievable. But why keep it locked? And what are all these things in here? Can I touch them?" Nikki's hands fluttered toward the box.

"Whoa, questions, questions. It's locked because other people can't be messin' around in my box. Everything has to be perfect, ready. And when I get more experienced, there will be poisons in here."

"Poisons!"

"Yeah. Like a little bit of something can be good, but too much can make you sick, or even kill you. Remember the chocolate cake at your little cousin's birthday? He sneaked extra pieces and got sick, and they had to get him to the doctor. He popped out in hives all over his body. Really. I was staring at his arm, and a red blotch popped up in front of my eyes."

Nikki laughed. "Yeah, poor kid. Too much chocolate can do it to you. But a little chocolate is on my personal food pyramid."

"As I said. Now listen, it's really important. This box isn't a drug store. There's cool stuff in here that can help make a sick person better. But that's only part of healing. The most powerful work comes from the spirit world and earth, from the mind and body, coming together in balance. A powerful healer can bring healing balance to a sick person, plus the right remedies. I want to be a powerful healer." Charlie-Chum looked up and caught his friend's eyes.

"This is serious, Chum. I'm proud of you. You will become a powerful healer, I know it," Nikki said, then gave her attention to the bags and bottles and tubes tucked into the chest. "Please, let me hold something."

"We'll empty out the box. Here, take this little vial of arnica oil, that's for bruises, muscle pains, sore feet. See, I gotta have all this stuff memorized. This one you'll love. Calendula cream, pretty yellow from the petals."

"What's it for?" Nikki unscrewed the cap.

"It settles down inflammations, sunburn, and skin problems. Don't know about zits, though."

"I think I've got a little sunburn on the back of my neck," Nikki said. "Could I try calendula cream?"

"Here, I'll put some on. I have to learn to doctor people." First he thanked the calendula that made the cream, and Nikki did too. Then Chum squeezed a dab onto Nikki's palm so she could see the beautiful color. She held her braids aside as he rubbed cream on the poor burned skin.

"Ahhh, feels nice, Medicine Man," Nikki said. They admired each item in Charlie-Chum's kit: cedar lotion, corn silk, echinacea capsules, echinacea–goldenseal salve, puffballs, sage leaves, slippery elm bark powder, sweet grass braid, witch hazel lotion, yarrow powder, yucca root. Then they packed all neatly back into the box, into the pillowcase, and under the table.

"What d'ya wanna do now?" Charlie-Chum asked.

"Everything!" Nikki said. So the two mixed all afternoon with tons of people, almost all were Mohawk family and friends,

15

plus visitors. Everybody danced and sang and talked. Chum got laughs for his jokes, and picked up a few new ones. They played a game, throwing spears at a moving target that was supposed to be a deer. That worked up an appetite, which they satisfied with traditional corn soup and corn bread hot from the oven. They rode into the woods on the farm wagon, squeezing with others on to wooden benches. Nikki moved up to the driver's seat next to her uncle, and persuaded him to pass her the reins. She drove the Belgian draft horses mostly around ruts and rocks in the dirt road. When she hit one, the wagonload yelled and laughed like they were on a ride at the county fair. Night fell and Charlie-Chum joined the men on stage, chanting songs, beating a small water drum made of a section of bass tree and filled with water, and shaking cow-horn rattles. The people listened to old stories told by the elders. Finally, an elder thanked the Creator and Mother Earth and every part of the natural world. He hoped they found the people had done a good job of loving and honoring Mother Earth and her great gift of strawberries, the first fruits of the season and very good medicine.

"We say thank you to Mother Earth and the Creator, and our mind is agreed."

"*Toh*," the people replied.

Way late that night, Nikki nodded off in the back seat of the old double-cab Ford F-150 pickup, as her dad drove them home with Mom beside him. Dad had to remove his headdress, called a *kastoweh*, 'cause it hit the cab roof when he climbed in. The *kastoweh* gave him an instant Mohawk hairstyle – it was a helmet made of wood splints and decorated with a ridge of deer hair and porcupine quills and hawk or eagle feathers. It was precious and had its own case for safekeeping.

Home was Northtown, on the river flowing into Great Sacandaga Lake. Charlie-Chum lived there, too, and they were classmates at the Northtown Central Junior–Senior High School. Chum rode home with his folks.

Dad swung into their driveway. Headlight beams caught a few steers watching over the pasture fence and made their eyes glow mysteriously. The lights continued in an arc across the gray-painted farmhouse and its fir-green window frames and trim. When Dad offed the ignition, motion ceased and that woke Nikki up. He opened the truck door for her, and she wended up the front steps and through the front door and upstairs to her room. Tired. Happy.

She gave her new possession a haphazard introduction to the eleven other polar bears that kept her company. Her clothes and moccasins dropped into a pile. Nikki pulled on plaid boxers and a chocolate-colored T-shirt, washed face and hands, brushed teeth, and left braids alone. She sighed into bed, along with the polar bear carving. She turned off the bedside lamp and dug down under the covers, her hand closed around the new guy. She was already slipping into dreamland. Bright snapshots of the day slid across her mind.

Then the bear growled, in her hand, right by her ear. Or Nikki thought he did. Her eyes popped open. Maybe it was a dream? No, this was real 'cause she was awake! She stifled a scream. The back of her neck crawled like she'd stepped on a snake. Nikki threw the bear on to her pillow, scrambled out of bed, and shook herself all over to get rid of the creeps. Then she switched on the bedside lamp. Every nerve stood on end.

The little woodcarving just lay there. He looked innocent, but who could tell? Nikki wasn't touching him, that's for sure. She grabbed a slipper, stretched it toward the bear and turned him so she could see his face. She had half a mind to throw him out the window.

"Growl again, bear. I dare you," she gnarred in her best monster voice. She felt foolish, talking to him and brandishing a slipper-weapon. "Where's my bear catcher when I need it?"

Apparently the bear thought talking was normal. He rumbled, only this time it sounded friendly, and Nikki understood the word, "Hello." She was plain shocked. She cocked her head, studying what to do.

"You won't hurt me if I touch you again?" Nikki was getting as deep into this as farm boots in mud. This time she understood all his words, though they still sounded like bear noise.

"Of course I won't hurt you, girl," the polar bear snorted. "You know I'm magic, you know I have a force field to keep you close to me, and you know the seer hoped I would take you to good places. Here's the deal: You and I, we are two. You need me, and I need you."

Now Nikki was more curious than creeped-out. She propped him against the pillow and sat cross-legged on the bed facing him. As they kept quiet, fear melted away and her senses rang clear as bells. She felt the polar bear's magic. The slipper got tossed to the floor.

"Why are you here, bear?" Nikki wagged her finger at him. "I want answers. And what's your name? I can't just call you 'bear' all the time."

"Very well, young lady. I've heard everyone call you 'Nikki' and I shall do the same. My name is Followme."

"That's a lame name, Followme. Am I supposed to follow you?"

"That's the idea, when we're on assignment for the Creator. We are two. How do you feel about that?"

Not so sure. "Does that mean you tell me what to do?"

The bear barked for a long time, which Nikki guessed was his way of laughing.

"I'm only here to give you wisdom and encouragement."

Good, but she had more questions. "Do I have a say in whether I take an assignment?"

The bear snarled with a warning edge. "Girl, who do you think you are? You would refuse the Creator?"

She shrank away from Followme. Such a quick change from warm mood to cold.

"I don't think I have what it takes, to work for the Creator." Followme made her feel out of control, like she was just sucked up by a giant riptide, strong as the one that got her at the beach two summers ago. She had screamed and a lifeguard swam out and saved her. One of those in a lifetime is enough.

Maybe Nikki should have screamed then. But her dad would wake up and come in and want to know was she having a bad dream. She didn't need Dad. Yet. So she let the Followme riptide carry her some more.

"No worries, young one. My spirit tells me you have what it takes for this mission: Courage to stand by your commitments, curiosity to try something new, and generosity to make all things good."

Huh. Nikki didn't know that stuff was so important.

"And you're a polar bear expert. Your character and knowledge make you more powerful than you think. You're almost ready for your assignment."

"What is this assignment?" *He said I have what it takes—* now she wanted to know if she'd like the job.

"Nikki, my girl, you are going to save the polar bears."

Riptide, take me away. "Fabulous. When do we start?" Really, she thought he was kidding.

"Hold your horses there, young lady. I said you're almost ready, but not quite. You need special abilities. You know what an *orenda* is, don't you?"

"Of course." She had been raised by her father to speak Mohawk and to know lots about Mohawk ways, though she wouldn't know everything until she got to be an elder. "An *orenda* is a spiritual gift. An *orenda* is sacred. You're not supposed to use it for yourself. You're supposed to use it for others."

"Exactly," said Followme. "You will receive two *orendas* from the Creator, through me. You already have one, though you won't think so until you try it out tomorrow."

"I do? I already have an *orenda*?"

20

Fifteen minutes ago Nikki was ready to slam this grumbling little figure with a slipper and throw him out the window. Now she was supposed to save the polar bears? And she already had an *orenda*? Hardly anyone had an *orenda*. She bit the inside of her cheek to be sure she was still awake. This stuff would make more sense in a dream.

"Indeed," Followme was continuing. "You are able to converse with animals. You can understand them and they can understand you. Like we are conversing now, magic polar bear and *orenda* girl."

"Stunning." Nikki's voice was faint.

"Tomorrow you will test your first *orenda*, and you will receive one more," said Followme.

"Tomorrow ... one more ..." she mumbled. Suddenly this was too much. Nikki's brain felt thick as oatmeal. First the excitement of the Strawberry Festival, and now all this crazy stuff with Followme. She thought he was just a nice carved polar bear. *Who knew?* Sleep. That's what she needed. She was tired.

"Followme, can't keep eyes open. Need sleep. You stay here." She put him on the wall shelf above the bed with her other polar bears. "Take a snooze." She keeled over, head-bombed the pillow, left covers in a bunch, and conked out.

CHAPTER THREE

TOO EARLY IN THE MORNING, Nikki was jolted awake by a sharp strike on the temple. She was dreaming about a bunch of crazy people, including her, climbing trees and throwing pinecones, and at first she thought someone got her good with one. The dream melted away, but the hurt place on the side of her head was still there.

"Ow!" She hated starting the day in a rotten mood. "Who did that?" she asked nobody in particular. As an only child she often talked to herself. Sitting up and swiveling around, she saw innocent-looking Followme beside her pillow. Nikki supposed he got himself to tumble off the edge of the shelf. Accidentally on purpose. She kept rubbing the bumped spot, frowning. But the bright day billowed into the room like curtains, and smells of breakfast tempted the girl to go downstairs.

"Okay, okay I'll get up." She gave Followme a rude poke. "But I'm mad. I wanted to sleep in after staying up late dealing with you." She thumped around, muttering. Followme didn't seem to care. He said nothing. Well Nikki didn't care about him either. Yesterday was weird, but that was yesterday. Now she was starting over.

Nikki pushed aside the blue-and-white checked window curtains and gazed out. The day was gorgeous. Now that she was up and washed and dressed, her feet wouldn't stay mad. Instead they sprang like Slinkies. She bounced downstairs and jumped the last three. No matter what that little polar bear said, she was going down to the stream.

Nikki found Mom in the kitchen, pouring herself a cup of coffee.

"You're up earlier than I expected, Sweetie, after such a big day yesterday." She added a drizzle of cream to the coffee.

Nikki kissed her mother good morning. "Yeah, it's such a pretty day I thought I'd tramp down to the stream."

"Excellent idea. I'm planning to garden. The corn's peeking up."

"Where's Dad?"

"Outside repairing the terrace, that place where the flagstones tilt and we always trip."

Nikki gulped a glass of milk, and built a fried-egg-and-Swiss sandwich on raisin bread to eat on the way. Tied to her belt like a pouch, a bandana held an orange and a snack bar. Hand on the back doorknob, she hesitated.

Surprising herself, Nikki pivoted and ran back upstairs. She supposed it would be all right to take Followme along. *How much trouble could he be?* She crammed him in with the orange and energy bar.

Zipping back downstairs, she was out the door with a giant glad breath.

"Hi, Dad!" she sang out to him.

"See you, Pumpkin."

This was her world. Running downhill across the back lawn. Scrambling over the ruined stone fence. Traveling the length of the big field, kicking through white doilies of Queen Anne's lace. Then she picked up sounds from the bandana, growls and grunts and rumbles. Getting louder—she had no idea that little guy could make so much noise, almost as loud as a real bear, or at least a cub.

Down on one knee, she untied the knot and opened the bandana.

"I'm getting beaten up by an orange," Followme protested. "You've got to get me out of here."

How could she stay mad at him? He was so cute, at least at that moment. Nikki lifted Followme out of his jail. *Now what?* He had a solution.

"Listen, since we are two, you and I must be able to see together and talk together. I would like to make a suggestion."

"Shoot."

"Tie me on as a necklace."

"Good idea, but I'm no jeweler."

"Where's your imagination, girl? Pull the leather lace from your boot. Tie me in the center, then knot the lace ends behind your neck."

This was pretty ingenious. When Nikki finished, the necklace positioned him high up on her breastbone where he wouldn't bounce with every step she took. The unlaced boot stayed on, just loose like a bedroom slipper. They continued, now two pairs of eyes observing what lay ahead.

Nikki picked up the stream at the field's far corner. During wet seasons, the rushing water here could churn with the power of a machine. Over the years, water had made a right good cut through the dirt, as deep as Nikki was tall. The family used a wobbly log as a bridge across the cut. Walking across was tricky, but she did it with her eyes closed, nevermind a loose boot. On she went, jumping off the end of the log, chugging up the hill, finding the path through the brush, and disappearing into the woods. On and on through the woods led the path, until it entered the silent, green hemlock forest.

This was Nikki's all-time favorite place and she never brought anyone with her. Hemlock trunks grew to the sky. Leafy green needles way up there cast green light way down here. It was a mysterious space, even holy. And in the hemlock forest, passing through its own ravine, the stream became a deep pool backed by a cliff. The place seemed ancient. Spirits of Mohawks who walked this ground a thousand years ago peopled Nikki's imagination.

"Thank you, Creator and Mother Earth, for this beautiful place, and for all the living things, animals and plants, and for the rocks and dirt and water and air and everything else we need. You give us life, and we give you thanks and love," she prayed. Nikki's grandpa taught her how to love Mother Earth.

At stream's edge, boots came off. The girl waded over the shale stone bottom. Water gave her a thrill of chill. It ran so deep that her shorts got wet. Her goal was a lichen-streaked rock the size of a car where she sat and stirred ripples with her feet.

She watched minnows flirt from nook to cranny on the stream bottom. Then her thoughts cut to the big deal about polar bear trouble: the Arctic ice is melting out of the polar bear's reach, and they need the ice as a platform for catching seals. *Ursus maritimus* can swim sixty miles or more trying to reach the ice, but he might swim in the wrong direction and never find any. Or a storm blows up and violent waves drown him.

"Followme, I saw a polar bear the other day on TV, and the TV people were talking like everything was normal. But it wasn't. You could see the bear's ribs through her fur. That bear was starving, but nobody paid attention. That's awful, if people can't recognize a starving polar bear. We seriously have to save those animals."

The question was how. Nikki needed to chew on this problem. She unwrapped the snack bar and munched to fuel her thinking.

Soon she realized the cold water was giving her brain freeze. She bet her lips were blue. Off the boulder she slipped and waded back to the bank, then monkeyed up a ladder of hemlock roots to reach ground level. The forest floor, centuries of fallen hemlock needles, felt soft and springy under bare feet. Her steps released a rich forest scent as she climbed to a favorite lookout. On the way, she demolished the orange that brained Followme, then sucked the juice off each finger and wiped them all clean on her T-shirt.

Now Nikki sat and sank into her naturalist's silence. Since before she could walk, her dad had been teaching her how to live in nature. It's traditional for Mohawks to know the woods and swamps and lakes and fields. Mother Earth asks to be loved in person, and for Nikki this was her favorite thing in the world, loving Mother Earth. Nikki relaxed her body and gentled her breath. She faded into the setting and began to observe. *What's happening today in Mother Earth's pool and forest?* Her eyes drifted across the pool and up the rock face, to the top of the cliff.

There perched a statue-still bird looking back at her, a falcon she guessed. The bird's breast showed a black-speckled whitish-toasty pattern. Nikki's fingers wanted to stroke it. She wished she could see him closer. She wished he would come down.

"Talk to him," said Followme, hanging around her neck. "Remember, conversing with animals is your first *orenda*. Try it, my girl."

Nothing ventured, nothing gained, she supposed.

"Hello, uh, falcon," the words tinny in Nikki's nervous throat. This felt like skipping the training wheels. She for sure didn't know how to use *orendas* the right way. *Are there even such things as* orendas? *They might be only as real as Santa Claus.* Yeah, she'd been conversing with Followme, but he's so weird that didn't count.

"Hello, girl," the falcon replied. He made chuk-chuk-chuk sounds with squeals of a rusty bike thrown in.

Sweet!

"You understood what I said?"

"Absolutely. You've got a sharp eye, to find me camouflaged up here."

"Oh, I'm a naturalist. I study everything I can about Mother Earth. Will you come down? Sit with me?"

"Why should I?"

"Because I want to know you, and I want to stroke your beautiful feathers. I won't hurt you."

"You won't hurt me? Girl, aren't you worried I might hurt you? Don't be naïve. Look at these talons." The hawk held up a foot forked with treacherous claws. "Look at this beak." He turned his head sideways to profile the powerful hook that finished his beak. "I'm a raptor. I kill and eat small creatures. And I can do a job on creatures not so small if the moment calls for it." He offered a creepy, beaky grin.

Nikki swallowed hard. How stupid could she be?

"Uh, falcon, will you promise not to hurt me if you come down?"

"Why should I?" parried the bird.

"Because I'm nice." *That sounded so mushy-mush. Nice? Bleah.* She remembered what Followme said last night, and tried again. "Because I'm generous. If you don't hurt me, and I don't hurt you, we can do good things together."

"Okay, I promise," he said, and swooped down, finishing on a fallen tree velvet-padded with emerald moss. He was a peregrine falcon, at home any place in the world. She'd never been this close to a falcon before—it was a privilege.

"Good," Followme said, though no one had asked his opinion. "Miss Nikki, I am about to bestow a second *orenda* on you, and this falcon will teach you how to use it."

"You're saying the three of us meeting here is no accident?"

"You are correct. No accident. Don't worry about it. My girl, grasp me in your hand."

She did, and was grasped in turn by Followme's magic force. It packed her with a solid, muscular power, like she had swallowed some amazing protein potion.

"Nikki, receive the *orenda* of flight."

"Say again?" She couldn't believe her ears.

"Nikki, you can fly."

His words made her feel dizzy, as if tumbling through the air out of control because she didn't belong up there. She let out a careful breath.

"Uh. Okay. I'm trusting you, Followme. How do I do it?"

Could she trust him this far? Up into thin air?

CHAPTER FOUR

"COME WITH ME," FALCON SAID from his mossy perch. "Just have your brain tell your body 'fly,' then jump, and you will fly." Without waiting for the girl to get tangled up thinking 'I can't,' Falcon swept his wings and mounted to the cliff top.

Here goes nothing, thought Nikki. She told her body, *Fly!* And instead of obeying gravity, her body took to the air. Simple as that. *Stupendous!* Nikki laughed out loud. Over the pool she flew and joined Falcon. A scattering of stone shifted off the cliff where her feet touched down. This was a miracle. She felt so light and free.

"Yay. I did it!" Nikki cheered. But then she had to sit down, because her legs wobbled like spaghetti. *Nerves,* she supposed.

"Guys, I love this, but it's extreme. I'm having trouble getting my head around the idea that I can fly."

"Leave your head alone, young one. Just let your body learn and enjoy the ride. I hear the view from the air is fabulous," Followme said. "I can't wait to see it."

"Okay, I mean to do this. I don't want the Creator to be disappointed in me. But someone needs to teach me the moves, and what to do about clouds and wind and rain, and all that stuff."

Falcon spoke. "I'll teach you. I'm an expert, as you must be aware."

Nikki's confidence made a welcome reappearance, now that she'd be apprenticing with Falcon. Her wobbly legs steadied. Her head didn't really care anymore that this flying thing was unrealistic.

"How does this work, uh, Falcon?"

"My name is Windemere Justis Peregrine, but you can call me Windy."

"Call me Nikki."

"Yes, I know. Followme told me."

Well of course he did. This play was already curtain-up. She was the new actor just coming onstage. Funnily enough, she was okay with that. These two seemed solid.

Nikki checked that Followme was tight in his leather necklace and she drew a happy breath. Adventure was hers. "I'm ready, Windy. Let's fly!"

Windy guided her over the hemlock forest, following the stream till it emptied into the Mohawk River. She slowed down to memorize this new view.

"Keep up, Nikki, keep up," Windy called back. He'd gotten pretty far ahead.

"The forest looks so different," she yelled. "I can't take my eyes off the treetops. Their texture's bristly and ferny and just gorgeous."

"That's nice, young lady, but you'd better speed up, or you won't be flying anymore. You'll be falling."

Uh-oh. Nikki put herself in gear. *Whoosh!* Down the river, currents stretched like long muscles. Across farm fields planted in ribbon-stripes, past cattle small and plump as raisins. A strip of highway led to town and they passed over the school. Busses packed into the parking lot like candy bars in a tray. Butterfingers. People walking in and out of the bank, the bakery, the barbershop could be tiny figures in a video game.

"You know what, Followme?'

"Tell me, my dear. How do you like your first flight?"

"I like it fine. It's amazing. But the world's so small from here that it looks breakable. It could be mashed by a giant foot or poisoned by a mad scientist."

"A lot is breakable. And you have a job of mending. The polar bears, I mean."

"Windy, is this how we'll get to the polar bears? By flying?"

"Precisely, in a day or two. For the long trip to the Arctic we'll fly high and fast. We can do a practice flight now if you want."

"Sure, I'd like that. How do I go fast?"

"Just think 'fast.' Stay close," Windy said, then shot outta there like a feathered rocket. In an instant Nikki caught up. Telling her body to fly faster was no different than telling herself to run faster. She streaked so fast her unfastened hair lifted

33

behind her like streamers. It didn't seem to matter where her arms were. The air held them up so they never got tired. She liked having them relaxed out to the side. Flapping like Windy was unnecessary. His flying was an amazing fact of nature. Hers was magic. She could even fly on her back or side. Surprisingly, she wasn't cold and she didn't have trouble breathing, even up this high.

Cotton ball clouds lay in their way—bird and girl cruised right through. Their shadows passed across Lake Champlain. Did any of the boaters notice that one was the shadow of a girl? Now the scene was like moving along a giant map. She knew the highway they followed north, out of New York State and into Canada. They tied a thrilling loop around Montreal on the Saint Lawrence River. The city looked like a science-fair model built by a kid with lots of patience. They continued along the Saint Lawrence, watching it belly into the North Atlantic Ocean. Nikki shrieked with excitement when she spotted a pod of white beluga whales. Windy didn't mind when she insisted on flying lower to see them. They zigzagged over the spot till she had her fill, then returned to cruising altitude and got home in a jiffy.

"Windy, that outclassed any ride at the county fair." Nikki tucked in her chin to see her little carving. "Followme, I'm so glad the Creator gave me this *orenda*. I feel like I was born to fly. I feel like my real self up here."

"Hearing you say that is music to my ears, my girl." They returned home.

CHAPTER FIVE

By NOW IT WAS LATE afternoon. Mom was home from working at the church's bring-and-buy shop. Nikki stopped in the kitchen to say hi and saw she was cooking lasagna. Nikki hugged her mom and rested close, loving that way, while Mom stirred her homemade tomato sauce. Mom was Italian, so they always had good things at the family dinner table. Nikki knew Dad wouldn't be home for a couple more hours. Either he'd be teaching at the university or he'd be working on a history of the French and Indian Wars—a lot of it was fought around here. Windy'd gone off somewhere. So for now it was just Followme and her.

Upstairs she lounged barefoot on her peachy-colored bedroom rug and giant lemon-yellow pillow. She glanced at the mirror attached to her bathroom door and stood up. It showed her medium tall and medium weight. Neither fat nor skinny. Nice chest. No hips, not yet anyway. Her low-rider shorts looked like a boy wore them. She couldn't do a girly walk. Instead she walked like an athlete, from soccer and canoeing. Just look at the soccer tan on the middle part of her legs, with pale skin where shin guards and socks and cleats go, and further up where the shorts are. Totally uncool. She got teased and hated it, but loved the sport. Her club team played almost all year round, so what was a girl to do?

What Nikki really wanted was to be both girly and athletic. The same way, she wanted to both look like everybody else at school and like the proud Mohawk she was. That's when she wore Mohawk jewelry or her hair in braids, and spoke Mohawk to the few other Mohawk kids at school. She did like the shiny black hair she saw in the mirror, rosy cheeks, tangerine nail polish on her toes. She wiggled them. All considered, not too bad. Except that she was a mess just now, having walked in the forest and flown to Montreal and whale-watched and all. Craziness!

She lay back down on the rug. Followme lay beside her. After all they'd been through, Nikki was getting attached to that little guy, like they belonged together, as the seer said. The two were talking polar bears again.

"Followme, I remember a story from when I was little. People say the story was handed down by Mohawks and other native people. This is a true story—our ancestors lived it, and science backs it."

"Once, thousands and thousands of years ago, our land was frozen in a great ice age. It was so cold that glaciers of snow and ice miles deep stayed all year round without melting. You could find warmer weather, like ours today, but it was way down south."

"Then an upsetting thing happened: the climate changed. I don't know why, but the weather warmed and glaciers began to melt. Followme, this is the part that reminds me of today. That was an olden-days global warming, and now we have another one."

"Around this place," she drew an imaginary circle in the air, "and even farther, it was all melting glacier. The story says the shrinking ice sheet was like a giant hand scraping ice and earth toward the Far North."

"Interesting, young one, to think of that old ice age. Interesting, indeed. The glaciers melted. What happened then?"

"Oh, this is the curious part. America had mega-animals in that old ice age like you wouldn't believe. Six-ton elephants, big camels, giant bison, great lions, huge cats with teeth as long as a hunting knife." Nikki jumped up to pull her nature encyclopedia off the shelf. "See, here are artists' pictures. Aren't they amazing?" She spread the book open where she'd been sitting and held the little bear up so he could see.

"The thing is, these gigantic animals pretty much died out when the ice age ended. The big ones couldn't handle the climate change. They couldn't adapt, so they disappeared. Plus, human beings hunted them, which made the situation even worse."

"So what does this have to do with our polar bears?"

"Don't you see? Polar bears are mega-animals. They're bigger than brown bears. They're bigger than anything else we have in North America. Now they're caught in the same life-or-death challenge—their little ice age is ending, so what can they do?"

She thought, then answered her own question. "What can they do? The old ice age has a message for polar bears: change or die." Nikki stared at Followme as she heard the words echo in her head: *Change or die.* A calm certainty locked in her mind. She jumped up and did a quick happy dance.

"Followme, I've got it! That's my job. I have to lead polar bears to change so they don't die." *Man, this felt good. It was a tall order, but where's the fun in life if you don't jump on the big challenges?*

Nikki's brain was firing on all cylinders. Snap, snap, snap. Everything she ever knew about polar bears and the Arctic lit up. Puzzle pieces fit. The impossible seemed rational. Followme and she brainstormed and came up with a plan. A few polar bears might randomly figure this out, but that would be too little too late. Their plan would help a whole lot of polar bears adapt and survive. But they needed Windy. *Where the heck was he?* Followme said not to worry, the falcon would be back soon, maybe even that night.

CHAPTER SIX

TICCAR, CHIEF OF THE POLAR bears, again read the report lying on his ice cube of a desk. The figures were worse than he had imagined. Good Ticcar sank his head into his paws and closed his eyes. He didn't want to see the truth, even though he knew perfectly well what it was. And he ardently wished he weren't the one to lead the polar bears through these calamitous times. Ticcar was afraid that more disaster lay ahead.

That's what Rollo, his chief advisor, told him. The numbers showed a healthy polar bear population until, suddenly, the last few years had brought a shocking record of sickness and death. Rollo sat on a chair carved of ice, facing the chief across his desk. Rollo was upset, and kept rubbing the arms of his chair. Going round and round with the black pads of his paws, the advisor polished the arms to the clarity of glass.

Lifting his head, Ticcar was mesmerized by the burnished ice. *Transparent as a crystal ball,* the chief imagined. "Now that's precisely what I need," he mused. "I would gaze into its mystery and divine what the future holds for polar bears, or even see what I must do to save us." Lacking a crystal ball, he fortified himself with a steadying breath, then ventured the question. He hardly dared speak it. "Rollo, tell me what you really think might happen to us."

"Sir, we are dying and not enough babies are replacing the adults. Polar bear life is at a tipping point. Like a seesaw, carefully balanced between up and down, between life and death. This is normal. But the horrible bringer of death we have among us is shoving the seesaw askew. When that happens, polar bears could disappear. Disappear! If you'll pardon me saying it, sir."

This was a tough thing to speak, and a tough thing to hear. Ticcar's chin drooped toward his chest and his back slumped, a picture of despair.

Looking at his chief Rollo continued, "Or, if the right changes are made, the balance can tip back from extinction toward happy days. Joyous polar bear times with many cubs and strong, healthy adults. Imagine! I believe this is still possible."

Hearing this, Ticcar seized a scrap of optimism. "I believe what you say. And I believe there is still time to act. 'Extinction' is not in my vocabulary; 'survival' is. Rollo, we must do whatever it takes to survive." Ticcar paused as a new thought presented itself. "The trouble is—no single polar bear can get that seesaw back where it belongs."

Rollo went even further. "I agree. In fact, I don't believe it's within our power at all, to tip the scale of polar bear existence from death back to life. We might make a few changes, but this

40

thing is bigger than all of us. We polar bears need help. And we need it now. We must trumpet the alarm all across the globe"

"Rollo, point made. This disaster is bigger than all of us. To start, please call polar bears in our territory to an emergency council, here, at the Ice House. We'll call it the Survival Council. And, Rollo, while you're at it, invite all the peregrine falcons. We'll ask them to carry this urgent news far and wide."

So Rollo spread the word. He sent five polar bear messengers out across the ice in different directions. Each of those commissioned five more messengers from the polar bears they met along the way, and so on. Soon thousands of polar bears heard the message, and those who were healthy enough started traveling to the Survival Council at the Ice House.

Having sent out the polar bear messengers, Rollo raised his face to the sky. He called out a sharp, summoning cry, a special sound peregrines understood, that carried far in the crisp air. Three times he called, and then he waited for a response.

Chief Ticcar needed the bears' peregrine friends to activate their avian network, which covered the whole world. It was imperative that the world learn about the polar bear disaster. Surely the world would help. People must help! Otherwise, Polar Bears might die out, memories of them remaining only in animal stories of olden days.

Ah, look! Rollo exclaimed to himself. Squinting at the sky, he detected several small dots, thousands of feet up. Peregrines are coming! Rollo's heart lifted with hope.

A dozen compact hawks settled down around Rollo. These birds were serious, thoughtful, and smart. And they had seen many things in many places. Rollo spoke. "Ladies and gentlemen, my dear friends. I deeply appreciate you answering my call. We have a serious situation here. Polar bears are getting skinny, babies are dying, and some bears can't make it through the tough times. It hurts me even to speak of this, but Chief Ticcar and I believe polar bears need help, or we will die out. Will you carry our urgent plea to humans all over the world?"

"Yes, of course!" "No question!" "Right away!" "What are we waiting for?" chorused the falcons.

"Rollo," Windy, spoke up. "I have a human friend, a girl named Nikki, who not only loves polar bears but is also magical. I think she should be at your Survival Council."

"Can she get here quickly?"

"Yes. As a matter of fact, this girl can fly. I'll bring her right away."

"Very good," Rollo said. "Please tell her she is especially invited. She must come."

"Will do."

Windy and the other birds rose effortlessly into the sky. Only the shush of wings lingered for a moment, a drifting feather or two, then they were gone. They would fan out in all directions, pass the cry for help to every other peregrine falcon in the world, and then to every pet in every human household and every animal on every farm. Those pets and farm animals would know how to speak to their humans. *Wouldn't they?*

For the present, Rollo had done his work. All of the messengers were on their way. Before long, polar bears would begin arriving for the Survival Council.

"And now," Rollo murmured to himself, "I must find some morsel of fatty meat to put in my stomach. I haven't eaten in so long that I'm afraid I won't have enough energy to make it through the council if I don't have a bit of food." Disconsolately Rollo shuffled away, starved shoulder blades poking up under his luxurious fur, in search of a seal.

Later that day, flying at blizzard speed from the Arctic, Windy alighted on the deck railing of Nikki's house and called for her. This was a couple days after the Strawberry Festival and Nikki was in her room, reading about the ecological threat. Catching sight of Windy outside, she invited the bird to join her through the open window. It took some persuading, but the falcon did flap up to the bedroom. He didn't exactly enter. *Who knew what dreadful thing might befall him inside a human dwelling?* He chose a safe position on the bedroom windowsill, neither in nor out. A patch of white pines stood a few wingbeats away, in case he had to flee.

"Hey, Windemere, how was your trip, what did you find out in the Arctic? Can we go help the polar bears right away? I'm so excited I can't wait."

"Trip was fine. Polar bear Chief Ticcar called a Survival Council. It is to be at their Ice House as soon as the polar bears can get there. You have a special invitation to attend. I told the chief's assistant, Rollo, you could help."

"What about the brown bears, are they prepared?"

"Yes to that, too. I explained our plan to brown bear Chief Wenobri, and he is ready whenever we are."

"Woo-hoo! Followme, did you hear that?" Nikki wiggled the leather string of his necklace to make the little polar bear dance. "When do we leave?"

"I'm ready when you are," said Windy.

"How about tomorrow morning?"

"Very fine."

"Listen, I want Charlie-Chum to come. One, he's my friend. Two, he's Mohawk so he loves Mother Earth and her creatures like I do. Three, he's learning to be a medicine man. He might collect interesting stuff on the Arctic tundra."

"That's fine, young one, except Charlie-Chum can't fly," Followme said. "How do you propose for him to travel?"

"Easy. We'll hold hands. My flight *orenda* will be enough for both of us. I know it. I have the willpower to make it be enough." Nikki looked at her two mates. She felt in charge. "Good, then. Charlie-Chum, Windy, Followme, and I will go save the polar bears. Our minds are agreed."

"*Toh*," all three affirmed.

"I gotta call Chum." Nikki untangled from her sprawl on the rug and grabbed her phone from the desk.

Windy said. "See you tomorrow. I'm going hunting. That little run to the Arctic and back drained my fuel tank." He exited the window and flew over the pines, out of sight.

Nikki speed-dialed Charlie-Chum.

44

"Hey, Nikki," Chum said, "Haven't talked to you since the Strawberry Festival, two-three days ago. What's up?"

"Lots. Meet me at the boathouse and I'll tell you everything. How soon can you be there?"

"Climbing on my bike as we speak. Fifteen minutes."

"You're not gonna believe this. Stoke up your imagination." Nikki hung up, zipped downstairs, and out the door, calling to her mother on the way. "Meeting Charlie-Chum at the boathouse, Mom!"

"Okay, honey! Be home in time for dinner."

She cycled toward their meet, standing on the bike pedals, pumping her excitement. *Was Charlie-Chum ever going to be amazed.* She laughed, picturing his face when she tells him. *This is gonna be rich.*

CHAPTER SEVEN

CHARLIE-CHUM WAS ALREADY THERE. HIS bike was atop the riverbank, tilted against the boathouse steps. Further down the bank, a weathered wooden pier ran straight out into the river, where the depth was about ten feet at the end. Small craft, canoes and stuff, could tie up to brass cleats mounted down both sides of the pier. Swimmers used the ladder at the end. Charlie-Chum sat on the pier, legs kicking back and forth in the air space between dock and river. Nikki sat down and mimicked him. Side by side, four legs kicking now. She shoved him with her shoulder. That was for hello. Twin smiles.

"Hey, I've got important stuff to tell you," Nikki said.

"So you said. Does it have to do with the polar bear? The one you've got around your neck?"

"Sure does. Listen. I'm going to the Arctic to save the polar bears!"

"Huh?" His head whipped around toward Nikki. He stared.

"I want you to come with me." Excitement bubbled in her throat, and she gargled the words.

"You want me to go with you to the Arctic to save the polar bears?" Chum repeated slowly. He got the words, but didn't understand their meaning.

"Yeah, that's it!" Nikki kicked faster. She was going places.

"Nikki, I know you don't make sudden, big decisions. You always think things through, right? So you're running way past me on this. How're you getting to the Arctic? Not to mention me. Polar bears are hungry. Why wouldn't they eat us when they see us? How would they know we mean to help? And how can we help anyway?" Charlie-Chum swung his head side to side. "No way."

"Way, Chum, way. Followme here gave me two *orendas*." She ticked them off on her fingers. "I can converse with animals. I can fly. Watch, I'll show you."

Nikki scrambled up. Charlie-Chum turned and watched. Nikki flew, and Chum's eyes widened. She snatched off his cap, one that said *Kanatsiohareke* for the name of their Mohawk community, and danced around in the air above his head.

"Hey, gimme back my cap. It's brand new, from the Strawberry Festival." Chum skidded to his feet and groped the air toward Nikki.

"Missed me," she sang. He grabbed and missed. She flitted toward the end of the pier. "Missed again." Chum tramped toward her, overshot, and fell into the river. Nikki carefully placed his nice, new hat on the pier, and jumped in too. They

48

horsed around and splashed and laughed. Out of breath, the two hauled themselves up the ladder and sat on the pier to dry out.

"Now you believe me, Charlie-Chum?" They emptied water from their sneakers.

"Now I believe you. But as a penalty for shaking me up, you have to listen to a joke."

"That is just and proper. Joke away."

"Okay. How can a person become attractive to a squirrel?"

"I never thought about it. How?"

"Climb a tree and act like a nut!"

"You are a wild and crazy guy," said Nikki. After a decent interval to appreciate his humor, she continued. "Chum, I'm serious. Come with me to the Arctic."

"When?"

"Tomorrow morning."

"That soon. How will I get there?"

"We'll hold hands, and my flying *orenda* will be more than strong enough for both of us. In addition to Followme—who knows the spirits and is a wise advisor—we have Windy, a peregrine falcon who's our scout and navigator. I thought you could bring your medicine knowhow. You might discover herbs and lichens and such on the tundra, kinds we don't have here."

"Tempting, Nature Nerd. But it sounds like we'll be away for months. My folks won't go for that. I'm surprised yours would."

"Probably they wouldn't, but they won't know. Followme says time will run differently. It'll be elastic. The Creator makes time, and can bend it. We'll be on a two-month adventure, but to our parents it'll seem we've only been gone a few hours. No big good-byes, no big worries. It's summer vacation, so no issues about missing school."

Chum stared at the fading daylight sweeping gold and amber on the river and spoke low. "Why me, Nikki? You're so on top of everything, you could do this mission on your own, seems to me. I'd just get in the way. Why don't you go, and come back, and tell me about it." Out of nowhere, he felt awkward, which almost never happened around his friend. But she was talking about things he couldn't imagine. Flying, for one. Getting shoulder to shoulder with monster polar bears for another. The exotic and alien Arctic for a third. He was sure he'd feel plodding and stupid.

"Why you. Are you kidding me? You're my longest and best friend. I used to say you're my best guy friend, but I really think you're my best friend of all. This mission isn't going to be a snap, you know. I'm so excited I'm about to bust, but I'm also so scared I can't think. I need you to keep me strong. You're steady, and you have a different kind of smarts from me. I think you would do anything to help, if I get in trouble. Same in reverse, you know that." Nikki draped an arm over his shoulders, and she felt his tense muscles soften. "Have I convinced you yet?"

"Yeah, you have. I'm with you, head, feet, and middle," Charlie-Chum said. The two sealed the deal with a smacking high five.

"Excellent. Prepare your backpack with all the usual stuff. Sleeping bag, tent. We'll forage and fish and trap, but we should

50

have a bunch of freeze-dried and dehydrated food. Don't forget water-purification tablets. First aid kit in addition to your medicine man kit. Bandanas. Hunting knife. Fishing gear. Matches and Zippo lighter. You know the drill. We'll each pack a book, then swap. Bring a deck of cards. Phone and solar recharger ... remember, no electricity up there. Clothing for wind and chill. Temperature might rise to the low sixties, but most of the time will be cooler. Rain? Could be."

"Yeah, I know, I know. How long have I been backpacking? Up in the Adirondacks, in all weather? Same as you, almost as long as I've been alive. Let's get going on this crazy adventure of yours." The two finished drying off on their bike rides home. It would be hard to sleep tonight, with secret adventure sizzling in their blood.

Next morning, Nikki kissed her mother goodbye. Dad was at work. "Charlie-Chum and I are going on a nature trip today," she fudged. Couldn't risk Mom stopping her, and what she didn't know wouldn't hurt her.

"With fully loaded backpacks? Looks like you're planning to be gone a long time."

"Not really. See you soon!"

"Have fun, Sweetie. Take your cell. Be home by dinnertime." Mom smiled at what an outdoorsy one that child was. Took after her father. *At least it's a healthy hobby, and Charlie-Chum was a good kid to share it with.*

Nikki clipped down the back steps, put on a sporty pair of sunglasses, and grabbed Chum's hand. They went around behind the windbreak of white pines, unseen from the house.

"Listen up, Charlie-Chum. On the count of three, we jump." Her friend was looking a little pale, but she figured he'd get over whatever was bothering him. Chum nodded ever so slightly. That was enough for Nikki, who counted them off. "Ready, one, two, THREE!"

With a jaunty explorer's grin, Nikki sprang into the air and along came Chum. He felt to her magically as light as a feather, which normally he was not. Windy was already airborne, gliding on currents, waiting for them. Nikki gained altitude, caught up with Windy, and the little party struck out for the Arctic.

"Wait, waaaaaaaait! Nikki!" Charlie started yelling as soon as the shock wore off. "This won't work!" Roads were thin as spaghetti below him. School looked like half a meatball. This was all wrong. He didn't belong here a-tall.

"Chum, don't you see, it's working. We're doing great." Nikki beamed a grin at him, which made him feel sicker.

"But what if you let go my hand? I'll fall to my death."

"Silly man, you won't fall to your death, because I will zoom down and catch you. Besides, I am not letting you go."

"That's all right for you to say. You're in control. I'm not. This handhold is not reliable."

"What would you like better?"

"I want to grab your backpack strap."

"Fine with me," Nikki shrugged. "It's fastened good and tight."

Whereupon Charlie-Chum began traveling hand over hand up the sleeve of her jacket, which made Nikki nervous. Turns out she was right to be nervous. When he got to the backpack, Chum got a better idea. Instead of grabbing a strap, he jumped entirely onto Nikki's back. It was a four-decker sandwich from top to bottom: backpack-Chum-backpack-Nikki. She screamed. The scream so startled Chum that he jumped and slipped off the side then grabbed Nikki from underneath. Now the two were face to face, screeching like barn cats. The wind made Chum's hair look like it was standing up straight. Or maybe it was nerves.

"Windy! Win-deee!" Nikki called. Windy, true friend, heard her cry and flew back to them. The whites of their eyeballs were showing, a condition the falcon hadn't yet seen in a human. He took charge.

"Come with me. We'll go down and get you two untangled." The falcon led the kids down in gentle sweeps and landed. The fliers slumped in the corner of a sunny meadow.

"Quiet, now," Windy said to Nikki. "Relax. It's okay. Everything's okay." It was the voice he would use to soothe scared falcon chicks.

"I don't think I can do this. Fly with you," Charlie-Chum mumbled, his eyes flat as dirty pennies. He hated admitting there were things he couldn't do, especially to Nikki.

Follow-me guessed his frame of mind. "Don't be troubled, young man." Nikki translated for Chum. "We'll have the two of you flying smooth as silk with smiles in your eyes. Just listen to me. Nikki will fasten me around your neck. I will endow you with the power of flight—as strong as Nikki's *orenda*—temporarily. Then nothing, absolutely nothing, can go wrong with your flying. You will conquer the skies. Do you believe me?"

Charlie-Chum nodded.

"Once the flight is ended, you will place me back around Nikki's neck. Under no circumstances will you fail to do this."

Chum nodded again.

Nikki fastened Followme around Charlie-Chum's neck. She leaned against him and felt the tension in his body. "Don't worry, big guy. I know you can do this. With Followme, flying will be a snap. Try it." Chum turned and she saw grave doubt flooding his eyes. "Go on, try it right here in the meadow. Jump, see what happens." She gave him a shove.

A reluctant Charlie-Chum stood, bent his knees, and jumped. His glad yell when he lifted into the air was a relief.

"Hey, Nikki, can you believe this? Followme, you're my guy." Crazy delight shaped his expression. He experimented, flying up, sliding down, looping around. Landing wasn't too smooth, but who cared? A crushing hug for Nikki, and a rub of affection for the wooden bear at his neck. Once again, Charlie-Chum was strong and brave and smart. "I'm set now. On to the polar bears!"

CHAPTER EIGHT

Despite the messy start, this time it was smooth flying. Windy sought air currents that pressed at their backs and propelled them along. Vast tracts of evergreen forest, *taiga*, signaled they had gained the Far North. On and on they journeyed. Nikki loved the rushing sense of her body in flight. From time to time *taiga* fell behind them to be replaced by gray-green tundra. Here tall trees were absent. The short vegetation, stunted by thin soil, rolled like carpet beneath them. Sunlight glinted on pools of water. Nikki knew they must be approaching polar bear territory, because tundra ended at the sea.

Windy confirmed her thoughts.

"Here's where we begin our descent. We'll fly past the shoreline, over a bit of sea, and finish on the nearest, largest ice floe. Watch for the polar bear Ice House. That's where the polar bear Survival Council will be."

"There, Windy," Nikki yelled, pointing. "Look, Charlie-Chum. Down there." At this distance the sparkly lumps she saw looked like a construction of sugar cubes. "There's the Ice House."

A few minutes closer, the scene lay below them in perfect detail.

Nikki gasped. "I never thought there could be so many polar bears together in one place, Chum. They're normally loners."

She was transfixed by the sight. Nikki had seen a couple of polar bears at the zoo. There, the wild creatures were on human territory. This was the opposite. The two humans were about to drop down into polar bear territory. The bears' wild rules would be the zoo bars for Nikki and Charlie-Chum.

"Look at all those black eyes and black noses pointed up at us. Who knew so many would come? Five or six hundred, would you say, Chum?"

"They're hungry. Won't they eat us?"

"I hope not," Followme muttered.

The polar bears spread out and opened landing space in the center of their crowd.

"We'll be surrounded by massed carnivores," Charlie-Chum yelled, forcing down the break in his voice. "Nikki, tell me we're not being fatally stupid." Why had he come? Nikki made it sound like a picnic, and that was all it took for him to say yes. *Dang!* He shouldn't be such a follower.

Though shivery hairs rose on the back of her neck, Nikki ignored her body's fear and Chum's worry, and made a skillful landing. Charlie-Chum hit the ice, but not on his feet. Anyway, he was down and safe. Normally, when meeting people, Nikki would smile. But she didn't think bears understood smiling, and they might even mistake a show of teeth. So Nikki just stood quietly before them, her face plain, and Windy on her shoulder. He was their badge of admittance. Since the polar bears trusted him, they must also trust them. She hoped. She reached out and grabbed Chum's hand, linking them together in Windy's protection. For his part, Charlie-Chum remembered Followme's admonition, and looped the magic bear back around Nikki's neck. This was going to be tough enough without sweating about losing his friend's talisman.

"Windy, stay with us. Please. Don't leave us alone here!" Nikki whispered. She refrained from making eye contact with any of the bears, in case that might stir them up. *Quiet bears, nice bears,* she mind-messaged to them.

None of the bears had rushed Nikki or Chum. So far, so good. But now two bears separated from the crowd and approached. One looked majestic, the other painfully skinny. *What could this mean?* They sized Nikki up as the leader.

"My dear Magic Girl," spoke the skinny one. "My name is Rollo, advisor to the Chief of Polar Bears, standing beside me. It is with intense happiness, and urgent hope, that we welcome you and your companions to polar bear territory."

"Uh, Mr. Rollo, thank you. I know polar bears are in trouble. My friends Windy and Charlie-Chum and I have come to try to help you survive. I hope this is okay with you and the rest of the bears."

The chief spoke. What he said made it clear he understood Nikki's mission. "Magic Girl, allow me to assure you we are eager to hear what you have to say. If you're tired, we can do this tomorrow ..."

A blast, like a shotgun in deer season, interrupted the chief. Nikki noticed the bears shifting nervously, looking and listening this way and that way. Chum looked nervous, too, and shuffled off.

CRRRAACKKK!!! That sound was directly under Nikki. She looked down between her feet and screamed. The warming ice floe they all stood on gave way in that instant. A canyon opened in the ice and Nikki fell in, screaming and screaming.

Down Nikki plunged, between ice walls and into the Beaufort Sea. The water was shockingly cold. Nikki was stunned witless. She sank through pale green water, weighed down by forty pounds of supplies. The further she sank, the deeper green the water became. *How many miles deep was it down there at the bottom of the sea, where the water was black as a polar bear's nose?* Nikki wondered in a panic. She was trying to hold her breath, but bubbles leaked out, and she couldn't remember how to swim. The backpack, clasps loosened once its bearer landed, slipped off and plummeted into obscurity, though Nikki was unaware.

Nikki was slipping into unconsciousness. She choked on water that was pressing to fill her lungs. In that moment, a strong water creature caught hold of Nikki and swam with her to the surface. Paddling over waves, boosting Nikki's head above the sea, powerful limbs lifted Nikki's dead weight onto the ice. The creature shook the limp body until Nikki coughed out water and drew in greedy gasps of air. Then the girl felt surrounded by warmth, and softness, and strength. Exhausted, she slept.

That is, she slept until her bear thought it was time for Nikki to come to. For that's who had saved her, a polar bear. The sow woke Nikki the same way she would bring a newborn cub to life: she lovingly used her large, grainy tongue to lick this strange but adorable cub all over her face. Nikki, startled, jerked around and opened her eyes at the rough treatment, just as a giant meaty blue tongue slurped her chin. *Phew!* Nikki pinched her nose. She didn't know polar bears had such stinky breath. The blue tongue was pretty shocking, too.

"Sea Bear, Sea Bear," Nikki whispered to herself, now restored. The face-washing was done. She was securely cradled in massive polar bear bulk. Curious, Nikki separated the bear's fur down to the skin. Yes! Polar bear skin really is black. Inspecting strands of fur, Nikki still couldn't see that each strand is a colorless straw, filled with warm air in the core. A giant paw reached down and scratched the belly, where Nikki had been exploring.

"What are you doing, young one?" the bear asked. "You are as mischievous as my cub was. Do you need to suckle? I still have milk, even though my adored little one just died. I couldn't find enough food for him, so he just withered away. My milk wasn't enough, you see, because I'm not eating well, either."

"Oh, my. I'm so sorry," Nikki said, stroking her bear's fur. "I didn't mean to disturb you. Your cub died? That's terrible," Nikki said, shaking her head. Tears oozed from beneath her eyelids. This assignment was becoming personal.

CHAPTER NINE

"THANK YOU FOR SAVING ME. I was about to drown," Nikki said.

"I never thought twice. When I saw you fall through the ice, I just jumped in. I'm used to swimming in this water; you're not," said the polar bear. "You can be my new cub. I will keep you safe and teach you polar bear ways. Would you like that, Magic Girl?"

"I would love that. But I don't even know your name."

"My name is Belinda."

"Very nice name. And instead of Magic Girl, just call me Nikki."

"Lovely. Nikki. Nikki my cub." A sweet expression molded Belinda's face.

"Will you oome with me to the Survival Council?" asked Nikki.

"Yes, indeed. And we'd better start now."

"Where's the boy who was with me? Did he take my pack?"

"What's a pack?"

"The heavy thing I carried on my back."

"What's a boy?"

"A boy is a human boar, a young one. Like, I'm a girl, a young human sow. We're too old to be cubs."

"I had no idea. I thought there were only boars and sows in the world. Now you tell me there are also boys and girls. As for your pack, the deep sea took it. You'll never see it again." Nikki's stomach flipped. Half the supplies were gone. But there was no time to think about that now. She had to find Charlie-Chum, and they had to get to the Survival Council. *Please, loving Creator, let Chum be safe and waiting at council, let me find him there.*

Nikki reached to her neck. "Followme. You're here! Are you alright?" Nikki unfastened the leather thong that held the figure in place and examined him. "You seem okay. A little soggy, perhaps."

"A little thing like drowning at sea can't stop your Followme."

"My faithful Followme." Nikki held him up to her cheek, then kissed him and strapped him back in place. "Belinda, I'm ready."

Belinda and Nikki had ended up a far distance from where she fell through the ice. They had to travel back to the Ice House. Treading across frozen whiteness with Belinda, Nikki worried that the ice might give way again. The horrible experience of hurtling between walls of melting ice looped Nikki into a powerful bond with the polar bears: melting ice was a death threat to all of them. This made the Survival Council even more important to her.

The two traveled over icy ups and downs. Sometimes, when Nikki couldn't resist the tempting slipperiness, she ran and skidded, ran and skidded, until Belinda urged her onward with a bump of the nose. Belinda loved it, because Nikki was acting like her cub.

Before long, Nikki and Belinda arrived on a broad, floating plain and the Ice House came into view. Nikki hurried and Belinda upped a gear to keep pace. The Ice House was as big as a university basketball stadium. The outside edges rose high in stepped peaks and pinnacles, surmounted finally by a giant central dome filled with windows. Bears streamed through multiple entrances, and Nikki rushed forward. There, black watch cap dragged down over his ears, was her friend. She ran, tears rolling down her cheeks, and jumped on him in a hug.

"Charlie-Chum! You're safe, you're safe. I prayed you'd be safe. I don't know what I would do without you."

Chum squeezed her back. "What would you do without me? Listen, I could never ever find another friend like you." Charlie-Chum loosened his grip to see Nikki's face, familiar as his own, yet strangely new in the near experience of losing her. "I thought you were dead, at the bottom of the Beaufort Sea. And not to be selfish or anything, but I don't know how to talk with these starving carnivores, and there's absolutely no way in the sky world or here that I could get home. I gave Followme back to you, remember? When you dropped through the ice, my life story turned to a short, sad end."

They unlatched, but couldn't let go. Arms around each other's waists, the pair let polar bear bodies carry them into the Ice House.

"Hey, Nikki, listen to this. What lies at the bottom of the sea and shivers?"

Nikki's eyes lit up. If Chum could joke, then all was well. "If it hadn't been for Belinda the bear, who saved me, that would be me. I would have lain on the bottom of the sea and shivered."

"Naw, that's not the right answer. Try again." He displayed a grin of relief.

"I don't know. Tell me."

"What lies at the bottom of the sea and shivers? A nervous wreck!"

"You crack me up," Nikki giggled.

"Good. Here, have a piece of bubble gum."

The assembly chamber formed a circular space, topped by the central dome. Ice peaks and pinnacles ornamented the inside space, as they did outside. Nikki sensed that the Ice House mimicked the round earth and the jagged ice of the polar bears' world. Windowpanes of the dome, thin sheets of transparent ice, let bright sunlight into the space. Bears sat all around the hall, leaving the aisles open for newcomers to enter. There were no benches. Back spaces near the exits filled more quickly than those in front, and the bears all sat cautiously far apart. Nikki got the feeling that polar bears weren't used to being close like this, and they weren't used to working in council. Suddenly it occurred to Nikki that, with too many boars packed in, fights could break out. Good thing she had Belinda for protection. She and Charlie-Chum wandered down the center aisle and found Belinda in the front row. Belinda placed Nikki and Charlie-Chum—whom she adopted on the spot, along with Nikki—on either side of her, sheltered by her bulk.

Nikki spotted Windy perched high on a windowsill as if it were the cliff he called home, alert and watchful. He coasted down.

"I've been to see the brown bears, making sure they're still ready for us, which they are. And I've been conferring with Chief Ticcar and Rollo. It's now or never for our experiment."

"This is good," said Nikki, stroking Windy's breast. But the raptor was restless, and returned to his elevated perch.

Charlie-Chum masticated the soft pink gum. He leaned toward Nikki across Belinda's belly.

"I don't like this setup. We're stuck in the middle of this arena, surrounded by 500 polar bears. Hear them mutter? What's it going to take to set them off?" A large pink bubble emerged between his lips for emphasis. It grew to the size of a grapefruit then popped, and he skillfully worked the gum back into his mouth.

Nikki huddled with Belinda. "She says everything will be all right."

"So how does this talking thing work? I hear you speak English to the bear, and she grunts and barks. Don't tell me she understands English and you understand bear."

"No, this is awesome. The *orenda* interprets. Belinda hears as if I'm speaking bear, and I hear as if she's speaking English, but we each speak our own language."

"Huh. Just don't forget that I don't have a clue unless you tell me what I need to know." Chum worked on another bubble.

"How could I forget you? Don't worry."

Just then two bears took up position in the center space. Did she remember them from when they first landed?

"We know these guys," Charlie said, leaning across Belinda. "They met us. Chief Ticcar and Rollo."

"Soon I'll be speaking," said Nikki. "I'm getting stage fright." The bubble she was blowing popped on her face. In Nikki's mood the sticky mess seemed to foretell what would happen when her turn came. *Please, good Creator, don't let me mess up.*

"I hope they can handle this crowd," Belinda spoke to Nikki, who interpreted for Charlie-Chum. He just rolled his eyes.

Then Nikki noticed that a pair of guard bears had taken up position at each aisle. Their beady eyes scanned the bears, who grumbled nastily.

Rollo felt the bears' sharp anger like a fish hook in the mouth. *Better move along.* "My friends," Rollo stood and held up his fore paws to claim the crowd's attention. "I am grateful to you for coming to this polar bear Survival Council. I know we bears aren't accustomed to working together this way, but emergency times call for emergency measures."

Rollo's voice was strong, but Nikki thought he looked unwell. His furry pelt drooped like a hand-me-down. Her heart went out to him.

Rollo continued. "The purpose of this meeting is to bring to light new ways that might save our lives. Actually, that might save polar bears as a species. As you know, we are dying, and we are not reproducing the way we used to. If we don't take bold action, then I'm afraid we have slim chance of a future."

As Rollo spoke, he looked at the crowd, bear by bear, hoping they would give themselves to this cause. As yet, he could not tell. Sullen murmurs laid a dirty floor beneath Rollo's words.

"Now, it is my privilege and pleasure to welcome our beloved and wise leader, Chief Ticcar."

Charlie-Chum leaned toward Nikki while she interpreted. "He's a chief. Better call him uncle, like we do with Mohawk chiefs at home."

Approving grunts brought Chief Ticcar to his feet, while Rollo slipped back. The chief struck a commanding pose. His imposing figure settled the crowd. Nikki saw that he was their leader, and he was trusted. His fur was glossy, his eyes were clear, his movements decisive. She wanted desperately for Ticcar to be the champion of the project that she and Windy were there to propose.

"I bet he's from the Bear Clan, same as me," Charlie-Chum said to Nikki.

"Is that a joke?"

"I wouldn't joke about that."

"My bears. Greetings. I don't think we have been together like this since I was made your chief many summers ago. Then was a hopeful occasion. Today is a frightening one. I know, because you have told me. Every family has been touched by death and struggle in the last few years."

This statement of fact caused a stir among the bears. Nikki heard them shout out their sad experiences. She scooted next to Chum, to interpret.

Ticcar listened with sorrowful eyes.

"My brother couldn't find a seal to eat," called out one bear, "so he tried to take on a whole herd of walruses. In normal times, he could have done it and been the victor. But hunger drained his strength. A bull walrus overcame him and gored him with tusks. My brother gave up. He just lay down next to the walruses and waited to die. They left him alone. Imagine! A polar bear no more threatening to them than a wee fish. I found my good brother's body after the life had gone out of him."

Another bear cried, "The snow cave for my babies fell in when the weather warmed, and the babies were so weak they suffocated. My poor little ones! What good am I if I can't be a mother and raise fine young bears?"

"My father washed up on shore, drowned," a perplexed voice spoke next. "We are Sea Bears. We shouldn't be drowning. But the ice melted so far out of reach that he couldn't find it, no matter how far he searched. He was near-starved, anyway, so he couldn't swim the distances he used to."

Another one piped up. "I tried finding food where the humans live. But a man came out with a black stick, and fire and noise came out of it. I thought it was coming to get me, so I ran away."

An angry voice added, "I've heard that humans made this horrible time for us. I've heard that their machines, all together, are very powerful. They send something into the sky that makes the sun burn our earth and melt our ice. We should make them stop."

CHAPTER TEN

"Everything you say is true, and none of it is just. These terrible things should not be happening to us," said Ticcar. "But, listen to me. It doesn't help to stand on our hind legs and bellow and claw the sky. Perhaps circumstances will change, a long time ahead. But right now we have a survival crisis. We polar bears must be smart and brave. We must act."

Ticcar viewed the assembly, taking their measure. *This just might work,* he thought. He stood and commanded. "Bears! We must act. I want you to commit to doing whatever it takes to survive. We have guests here who will help. But first I want to know: Will you commit yourselves to survive?" Ticcar heard scattered voices. He wagged his sleek head. "Not good enough, my friends. Let me hear you: We Will Survive!" He punched the air with his paw.

"We Will Survive! We Will Survive!" the council shouted back. "We Will Survive!" Full-throated roars filled the spherical space like a living thing, thick and muscular. Nikki knew this was good, but she shook in her socks, so mighty was the sound. Charlie-Chum choked and swallowed his gum.

"Maybe we should get out of here, Nikki," he yelled over the din.

"No, no, it's okay," Nikki grabbed his arm. "The chief has them committing to survival."

Ticcar sat down, and Rollo replaced him. It took a long time for the crowd's energy to smooth out. At last he could be heard. "Listen! Now we're committed, let's have ideas for survival." The crowd respected the chief's assistant as a thinker. They quieted. "This is going to require us to think in new ways. We polar bears could experiment over time with new ways to survive, just because we're hungry. But we don't have time to wait for lucky experimenting. We're smart. Let's think."

Nikki leaned toward Charlie-Chum. "Polar bears are extremely intelligent, you know. This will be interesting. They're coming up with ideas for survival. It means they'll have to change behavior. Tough." Chum shook his head.

"I've been thinking," offered the first bear to speak, "that my brother wouldn't have died, and he would have had a good meal of walrus, if he hadn't been hunting alone."

"But we polar bears always hunt alone," several objected.

"Right. That was fine, before. Now we hunt alone, and we starve alone. Think how unbeatable we would be if a pawful of us hunted together! But we would have to share and not fight."

"That's not in our nature," many bears said.

"It could be. I'm ready to try. Any others who want to group hunt, see me after council," he ended.

The mother bear who had lost her babies when their snow cave collapsed had an idea. "When I lost my babies, I still had a little milk coming in. I know that lots of mothers have sickly cubs because they can't supply enough milk for them. What if I could give my extra milk to some hungry little ones? It would make me so happy! The cubs would grow strong, and my milk wouldn't be wasted." Mother bears agreed to meet after council to give this idea a try.

"I want to keep going where the humans live," insisted a boar bear. "They throw food away, and sometimes I find good stuff. I've also been thinking about killing their dogs for food."

"But won't the humans kill you?"

"I don't think so. Mostly they try to scare me away. So I go when no one's around. But I think they might get really mad if I eat a dog. And I know they would kill me if I attack a human."

A few younger boars liked this idea and thought they would try it.

Another bear said, "When I'm hungry I sleep a lot. I'm thinking of sleeping longer this winter. If I'm asleep there's no need to hunt."

Then a loud voice crashed down. It set Nikki's teeth on edge. "Well you go ahead and sleep, you flabby no-good excuse for a polar bear," snarled the biggest bear of them all. He reared up on his hind legs. Nikki was blown backward by his size. She thought this boar could be ten feet tall. She bet he weighed a ton. Really.

Belinda shifted, shielding Nikki and Charlie-Chum so as not to attract the giant's attention. She whispered to her new cubs, "Ssorog has no match in all of polar bear territory. He and Ticcar fought it out for leadership of the polar bears. Ticcar's courage and smarts were a close match for Ssorog's power, but in the end Ticcar lost the fight. You can still see scars on his face. Though Ssorog won, he has few friends. Instead of him, we chose Ticcar as our chief. But Ssorog still carries a hot grudge against his opponent. In a way he blames everyone because he isn't chief. We never know when he will explode." Belinda stopped. Ssorog was bellowing again.

"Now me," Ssorog said, "I'm hunting and fighting and sinking my teeth into hot red meat anytime I can. Any living animal better run scared from this polar bear." It was both a boast and a warning.

Ssorog turned his head this way and that way, smelling something, seeking something. He found it: two tender juicy young humans, sitting across the hall. "GGRRRAaaAAHH-hhhh!" Ssorog roared. "What are those humans doing here? Humans are our enemy. They make the ice melt. They are the cause of our misery. These youngsters should know polar bear fury, and I'll show it to them. Get out of my way."

Ssorog galloped full speed across the space toward the kids. Thinking fast, Nikki grabbed Chum, sprang into the air, and flew up to join Windy. On a windowsill near the domed ceiling, they were far out of Ssorog's reach. The giant was furious that his quarry had escaped. He began beating up bears near him just because he was mad. Belinda moved out of the way and kept her eye on Nikki and Charlie-Chum. *What a surprise those cubs are,* Belinda's expression said.

"Heavy duty, Nikki," Chum gasped out. "That was a choke-hold you had on me." Chum stroked his sore Adam's apple.

"Sorry, Chum. Thank you, Followme. I heard you say 'window.'"

"Well done, young lady."

"Here, Chum, put Followme back on, in case we're separated, and you have to get away."

"Hi, Followme," Chum said as he looked the little guy in the eye. "I'm glad to be back with you again."

"Likewise, young man."

As big as Ssorog was, it took about ten boar bears piling on top to make him settle down. Ssorog's violence took the energy out of the discontent simmering among the bears. The company settled down, and Chief Ticcar invited Nikki to come to his side. Still frightened to her toes, Nikki bucked up her courage and slipped down to Ticcar. She wasn't going to let fear ruin her mission. Ticcar enclosed her in his strong arm and whispered that she would be safe with him. Nikki saw that Ssorog was now seated near a doorway, surrounded by guard bears. He couldn't harm her here.

"Now, my bears," continued Chief Ticcar, "we have very special guests visiting our Survival Council. They have something important and exciting to propose. Please give your full attention to this human. I call her Magic Girl, but her name is Nikki. With her is a peregrine falcon we know: Windy, our good friend; and Charlie-Chum, a medicine boy. The boy is up in a window," Ticcar gestured. So funny was the sight of a human on their windowsill that the bears enjoyed a chuckle for the first time this day.

Ticcar remained in the center space with Nikki. Windy, perched on her shoulder, provided the strength of his presence. His claws were sharp, but he grasped her gently. Nikki had imagined this moment, but her imaginings had not prepared her for the reality. She had been in polar bear land only one day, and already one polar bear had saved her life and adopted her, while another had tried to kill her. She had not expected the bears' feelings toward her to be so opposite, so powerful, and so unpredictable. Nikki looked out at the half-thousand polar bears and studied their expressions, all focused on her small self. In a panic, Nikki thought that maybe this had been a horrible, stupid idea for her to think that she could help these polar bears. Nikki wanted to fly as fast as she could back home.

But then, as she looked again at these magnificent creatures all waiting for her to help them, her heart and soul stretched out to cover them. It didn't matter whether they liked or disdained her, Nikki was going to try her best to help polar bears survive. After all, she had Windy, Chief Ticcar, Belinda, and Charlie-Chum on her side for a good start. And now she already knew what it feels like to have a monster bear galloping toward her like a truck, gigantic teeth bared, intending to make a meal of her. She knew how that feels, and she also knew that her instinct to fly away would save her. *So what more was there to fear? And if she didn't help the polar bears survive, who would?* Too many people think the bears' extinction is inevitable. But Nikki didn't believe that at all. Here she was on a mission. She would not back out.

Nikki was steady. She was ready. But she didn't know how to start.

"Windy, what should I say?"

"Ancestry."

"Ancestry?" *That's strange,* Nikki thought. *Okay, let's try it.*

"Hello, bears. You've never seen me before, but I love you. I live down south, where there are no ice floes. But I know about polar bears, and I know you are amazing.

"I am thinking about ancestry. I don't know if you use that word. Ancestry is all of your family that lived before you, going way back in time. I bet you will be surprised by this: going way, way, way back in time you and I are related to each other. Humans and polar bears are cousins! We all have fur—well, this is my fur," Nikki said, holding up handfuls of her long black hair. "And I have very thin fur on my arms and legs." At this, the polar bears all laughed and rolled around with hilarity.

"Yeah, tell us another one, Nikki," they yelled. But Nikki was encouraged, because now the bears were laughing. So much better than fighting.

"Okay, here's another one. Humans and polar bears give birth to live babies. We don't lay eggs," here Nikki glanced at

Windy "like, for instance, peregrine falcons do. And our mothers feed their babies with milk."

"Huh, that's true for us. True for humans? Who would have thought," the polar bears said.

"We have some other things in common. A big one is this: Polar bears and humans are omnivores. We can eat anything—plant or animal. I know you think of yourselves as carnivores, meat eaters, but you can eat other kinds of food."

Ticcar had said they would have to think in new ways, and right at the start they were. Not eat meat? That sounded pretty awful, but maybe worth a try. Better than starving to death.

"So to begin, we have common ancestry. We are cousins, polar bears and humans. If you are in trouble, then I'm in trouble, too. Will you accept help from a cousin like me?"

"Yes, yes we will," the polar bears said.

Nikki turned around and looked at Ticcar.

"Go ahead, you're doing well. They're with you," he said.

Encouraged, Nikki continued. "Now let me tell you something about my ancestry that is different from yours. My people are called First Americans, because we were the first humans in this whole big land of America, including here."

"Now, listen to what my First American ancestors knew, and told us. Long ago there was an ice age, and it ended. Giant animals, some bigger even than polar bears, lived in that ice age. Then the ice pack melted down south, and those big animals didn't know what to do. They were stuck in their old ways. They couldn't find the food they wanted to eat anymore. Some of the little animals survived, but it was hard for the giant ones, the mega-animals. For the mega-animals it was change or die. And most died."

Nikki saw the polar bears slumping now, looking discouraged.

"This ancestral story is like your story right now. The ice is melting, your usual food is disappearing, and the mega-animals—that means you—are dying."

"Why did you come here to tell us that? That we're all going to die, like the mega-animals before?" whined several polar bears.

But these polar bears were silenced by the wise ones in the council. "No, you've missed the point. Nikki told us her ancestors' story so we can have a different story. We don't have to die. But we do have to change. Food is the main thing, so we must learn to eat something else besides seals."

"Why do we have to be the ones to change?" one bear pointed out. "Humans brought this upon us—humans should change to roll back environmental warming."

At this point, Chief Ticcar spoke. "You are right, my friend. Humans have caused this problem, and we hope they will come together to correct it. But in the meantime, what Nikki tells us is the plain truth: We must do things differently. Now, frankly, this excites me, because I think we can do it. We polar bears are smart enough to change our ways. Let's use our heads!"

"The ideas you came up with before—group hunting, nursing helpers, and hibernating longer—are good ones, and we should start on those right away. I'm not so sure about scavenging food from humans; it sounds very risky. It might be more death-dealing than life-giving. But if you feel you must go to the humans, I won't stop you."

"Plus, I believe Nikki has an even more thrilling change for us to consider." Ticcar quizzed Nikki with his eyes, and she nodded. Once again Nikki claimed the space.

CHAPTER ELEVEN

"THANK YOU, UNCLE. OKAY, YOU guys." Nikki was getting the hang of talking to these bears. "We're still talking ancestry. First, I explained that polar bears and humans share ancestry. You and I are cousins. That's why I love you and why you should love me back."

"Second, I told you about my ancestry as a First American, and passed on to you a true First American story that says you must change or die."

"Third, I have something very interesting to tell about polar bear ancestry. Are you ready?"

By now the bears didn't know what to expect from this girl, but she sure was entertaining. Nikki caught a few rolling eyes and a few raised eyebrows.

No matter. She was on a roll. "Do you polar bears know anything about brown bears?" Nikki asked. The bears responded with nasty growls.

"They're ugly!"

"Yeah, with those dish faces and humped backs."

Nikki was shocked by the intensity of the criticism. Either the polar bears hated or feared their neighbors. Maybe both. She shook her head with irritation. How self-centered.

"Well, given your attitude toward the brown bears, you probably won't be happy to learn that you and they were once on the same branch of the family tree."

Now the polar bears were in a tumult.

"You're just telling lies."

"Couldn't be. Polar bears and brown bears are just plain different."

Nikki just put her face in her hands for a moment. This was turning into a mess. Like her bubble gum. How could she persuade Polar Bears to try the experiment she and Windy had in mind, if they couldn't see brown bears as kin?

"All right, all right, let's calm down. Don't get all worked up. It's not important. Just forget what I said about the family tree," Nikki soothed. "Let's go on to the big experiment: Polar bears change to survive. This is really big. Really exciting."

"Okay, okay. Tell us the big thing," said the polar bears, willing to listen if it could mean their survival.

"It does involve brown bears, and you will have to be nice to them. Can you do that?" asked Nikki.

A lot of low growling sounded like annoyance ranging to disgust. But a few bears said, "If there's a good enough reason to be nice, then we can do it. Tell us more, Missy."

Then Ssorog bellowed from his seat far away, "Nothing good can come from a brown bear. This skinny human cub wants to hurry our death. She says she loves us, but she really wants us dead! It's a human plot to wipe us out."

At this accusation, Belinda began to wring her paws. She knew her cub Nikki from a mother's heart. No way on earth could Nikki mean harm. Besides, everyone knew Ssorog was a bully and a liar. Surely, thought Belinda, the bears would bark him down.

But that's not what happened. Now the bears were confused. Could Ssorog's accusation be true? Who should they listen to? Their worried grumbling was beginning to turn angry.

"It's a plot, I tell you," Ssorog continued to bellow, "and if Ticcar brought the girl here, then he's part of it."

"Why would humans plot to destroy polar bears?" the bears worried out loud. They understood little about humans. "And why would Chief Ticcar help?"

"It's simple, you bumpkins. If we're not here, then humans can do whatever they want with polar bear territory. They want to dig our land up. And they want to break the ice and run boats."

Now horror sounded in the bears' growls. They could believe this, because they had seen the digging-machine monsters, and had seen bigger and bigger boats channel through the ice.

"Plus," continued Ssorog, "I bet our chief's got a deal to live fat and happy in a zoo down south. Along with a lush lady," the trouble-maker sneered.

Nikki was truly astonished by this accusation. She knew from Belinda that Chief Ticcar was beloved by his polar bears. He had always been a wise, courageous, and sympathetic leader, and he was always a gentleman with the ladies.

But under these circumstances, the bears were steeped in fear. Nikki could actually catch the rancid smell of it. They were inclined to believe anything, no matter how crazy, that stirred up their fear. The more bears that yelled together, the stronger they felt. And Ssorog was their champion. He understood them. His leadership would be harsh and muscular. They would be winners again.

Belinda intervened. She stood up, and raised both forepaws in the air to call for silence. Belinda was esteemed as a good mother. The crowd, almost out of control, sat down and quieted. Belinda was probably the only bear who could have this effect.

"Now you listen to me, you bears. You're behaving like adolescent ruffians. What would your mothers say? In fact, I see many mothers here—about ready to give you a good cuffing for this ugly behavior. Polar bears are better than this. Forget Ssorog; he's only interested in Number One. Instead of struggling to survive, that bear will drive you to self-destruct. Do the right thing, the intelligent thing. Listen to Ticcar, our true leader, and this Magic Girl who loves us. I don't know what it is, but I think we are going to discover a real chance to change and to survive."

Nikki's adopted mama sat down, and it was clear to Nikki that the mood of the council had changed. The energy that Ssorog had charged now coursed in a different direction, right toward her. Ticcar they knew; now they wanted to hear how she, Nikki, would lead them.

"Thank you for listening to me. First of all, I am not plotting against polar bears. You've got to believe me! I'm here only, only because I want to help you survive," began Nikki.

"I want a group of you to be pioneers. We will walk together away from the ice. We will travel to places where there is more food than you can imagine. Delicious food that polar bears can eat and be happy. Doesn't that sound good?" asked Nikki.

"It sounds wonderful," a bear said.

"My tongue is hanging out, just thinking about all the food," said another.

"What's the catch?" asked a skeptical bear.

"Okay. You're right, there is a catch, if you want to look at it that way. Or, you can look at pioneering as an adventure. Here's the adventure: You won't be eating seals. You will eat very well, but the food will all be new things."

"Awww, I don't want new food. I want the same old, same old stuff," several bears complained.

Just like a lot of humans, thought Nikki. *Kids especially. Some will only eat five or six things, period.* Nikki always thought that was babyish. Well, she wouldn't say that to the bears.

"I know you like seals. It's the food that polar bears always eat. But, you hunt seals on sea ice, and the sea ice is melting, so it's much harder to get to the seals. And who knows? You might find some lip-smacking new food when you pioneer," coaxed

Nikki. "Here's what we'll do," and Nikki proceeded to lay out plans for the pioneers.

"We will need about thirty volunteer polar bears to be pioneers. We will be away from summer to summer, maybe longer. That is, except for me and Charlie-Chum. We'll have to go home when summer ends," said Nikki.

"Understood," said Chief Ticcar. "I will lead the pioneers. Nikki and Charlie-Chum and Windy will be my advisors. I believe this experiment is essential to polar bear survival, and I will do anything for its success. Meanwhile, my dedicated assistant, Rollo, will remain at the Ice House to keep up with affairs. Thank you, Rollo," Ticcar said, nodding toward his right-paw bear.

"You are most welcome, Sir," Rollo said, then sidled away as he went into a fit of coughing.

"Now, before any of you volunteer," said Nikki, "I must tell you about the other catch. Ready?" The bears were silent.

"Your pioneering destination will be ... brown bear territory. You will be their guests, and they will teach you all they know about living in forests and meadows, on tundra, along rivers. What brown bears eat, polar bears can eat."

At this, there was an uproar.

"I don't believe it," one bear protested. "You know we hate brown bears. Why would we be their guests? And let them lord it over us, being all superior, showing us their awesome hunting and scavenging techniques?"

"Just the idea makes me want to barf."

"I bet you, Chief Ticcar will tell us we have polar bear honor at stake. That we can't be rude or get into fights or any of that."

"Come on, fellas, think positive. Maybe you'll make friends. This could be good. Plus, our ladies, our sows, may find some boars to their liking. The other way around, too," Ticcar said, with a smile on his black lips. "Now, besides Nikki and Charlie-Chum and Windy and me, who else will be a pioneer?"

"I will," said Belinda. "I must be with my cubs." *This was so sweet,* Nikki thought. She shuffle-slid on the ice over to Belinda and leaned into her side.

Some other mothers with cubs volunteered. A few sows hoping to find good-looking, good-hunting boars to mate with. There were also teenage bears, three to five years old, who thought pioneering sounded like the most awesome thing ever and insisted on going. A number of boars filled out the group. Ticcar was quite satisfied.

CHAPTER TWELVE

THE POLAR BEAR PIONEER POSSE paddled from ice to shore. Nikki and Charlie-Chum flew over. Chum had the remaining pack strapped fast to his back. He would never take it off, except in camp, wherever that turned out to be. Everything he and Nikki had to keep warm and fed was in there. Big trouble if something happened to it. Nikki stood beside him on the beach, watching the sopping bears mill around, her expression flat as a cold stone. *She could get so serious. Better lighten things up.*

"Hey, Nikki." She looked at him.

"What did the polar bear say to its mother at mealtime?" He watched one side of her mouth quirk up, not quite a smile.

"I don't know. Maybe 'I'm hungry, Mom.'"

"Nope. 'Awww, not seal again!'" Nikki laughed in her chest, and she smiled, but just with her lips, which were chapped. Chum handed her the lip balm from his warm parka pocket. He could tell she was dead tired. No wonder, either. They hadn't had proper sleep since leaving home. That seemed like years ago. "You tired?"

"Yeah, sure. We'll rest up soon." She handed the lip balm back.

Charlie-Chum continued to study his friend. Most times he could tell when something was bothering her. She seemed real heavy to him just now. "What's going on with you? Tell me."

Nikki held him with a clouded gaze. "Chum, I can't do this."

"Can't do what?"

"Help the polar bears."

"What do you mean? We're here, you're helping them."

"Not really. The thing is, Chum, I can't get close to them. I don't want to feel their suffering."

Charlie-Chum gave a slow shake to his head. "You're nuts, Nikki. Who cares whether you feel their suffering? Look, you've already accomplished the toughest thing, and that's getting these lunks off their hindquarters. They're going to try living a new way. That's huge."

"You remember when my grandma was sick and dying, last year?"

"Yeah, I went to her funeral. I always wondered why you weren't there."

"I wasn't at Grandma's funeral, and I didn't visit when she was dying. I was so scared of her suffering and petrified of her dying. I loved her to pieces. But I was afraid if I got close, her suffering would drown me. I was gutless. Everyone thinks I'm great, but inside I'm a selfish coward." While Nikki spoke, she kicked a trench in the beachy gravel. "I didn't tell my grandma I loved her. The last thing she knew, I abandoned her. I think I'll feel guilty for the rest of my life. And when I get close to other suffering, my guilt over Grandma comes back."

Charlie-Chum shrugged. "I still say it's no big deal. Just get over it. This is an adventure. You like adventures, don't you?"

"You know I do."

"Well, then. To adventure!"

"Yeah. If you say so."

Belinda came over and said it was arranged: Ticcar would lead, and Charlie-Chum would ride him. Belinda would be last, to keep track of stragglers. Nikki would ride her. No flying for the kids, because Nikki wanted to experience the pioneer trek at bear level. Charlie-Chum glanced over and saw Nikki's jaw set. *She was going to carry on. Good.* Chum grabbed onto Ticcar's fur and flung himself onto the beast. He scrunched around and made a seat for himself, just behind the bear's shoulders. *Man, this was weird, riding a mighty polar bear.* But he felt pretty safe, now that he knew Ticcar. Chum thought of him more as a protector, than as a carnivore who might at any second bite his head off.

The bears were underway when one last boar, dripping wet from his swim, gallumpfed up to the group and braked to a stop in front of Ticcar, blocking the way. Belinda saw the late-comer rush past. It was Ssorog.

"Hold on, Nikki," Belinda barked. She sped off at a lumpy gallop to the head of the line, where Ticcar was. She didn't want that bully to journey with them. He was nothing but trouble. Nikki plastered herself flat on Belinda's back and screamed at the thrill of riding a galloping polar bear, though the scream felt like grief. She could not banish from her mind's eye the image of her grandmother in a misty distance, back turned to her grand-daughter in final reproach.

They caught up with Ticcar just as Ssorog said, "I'm going with you." It was not a question, but a statement of fact. Ssorog and Ticcar regarded each other coolly, rivals still.

"If journeying to brown bear territory opens the new age for polar bears, then I am there. And I intend to be the best. You have any problem with that?" he demanded of Ticcar.

"No problem at all," Ticcar said. "We need strong polar bears to survive. And we need smart bears, who know when to fight and when to get along. I know you're strong. Are you smart?"

"You will see what I am," said Ssorog, aggressively dealing an ambiguous answer. "I will prove myself."

"Then I will expect the best."

Windy swirled in front of the little group, then led them onward, further across the tundra, the sea at their backs. Belinda with Nikki returned to the rear, while Ticcar lumbered ahead with a polar bear's rolling gait. Charlie-Chum tried to figure it out. Ticcar's front feet turned inward, pigeon-toed. First stepped the right front foot, followed by the left hind foot, then the left front foot, and last the right hind foot. Chum groaned. *Of course polar bears wouldn't walk the way other animals do, two feet at a time, nice and steady.* He tried to get used to it, but felt like he was helpless on a small boat in a heaving sea. His stomach was not happy. Becoming a little green about the gills, he tried to steady his world by fixing his gaze on the immoveable horizon, and in this way Charlie-Chum began studying the tundra that swept before them.

He saw the land was flat, but changeable. In the distance he noted small mountains, vegetation clinging to sunny slopes like honey coating a spoon. *Were those trees?* Somehow he doubted it. Everywhere around him, the severe arctic climate forced plants into a protective crouch. Save for the greened slopes, the mountains appeared to be heaps of bare rock. He would see. He bet that up close he'd find small plants dug in, even on winter-beaten rocks. On the flat, where they traveled, thickets of shrubbery blotched the land, and broad sweeps of greenery and flowers painted the thin ground. Summer sunlight washed the scene in pink and blue, green and gold. Charlie-Chum liked it, and couldn't wait to explore. The bears were poking along, then resting, poking, resting. He could walk to the mountains and back, before the bears would get where they were going. He might as well go see what secrets the tundra held.

Next time Chief Ticcar stopped, Charlie-Chum rolled onto his stomach and slid off. "Bye, Uncle. Thanks for the ride." Of course, the bear had no idea what he was saying, but Chum was raised to be polite. It couldn't hurt. Shaking the backpack into place, he strode away, boots crunching the thin soil. He fell into a steady hiker's pace and sucked in gulps of fresh air. Felt great. Now he was on his own terms, not cooped up with polar bears in a crazy, giant igloo. Charlie-Chum covered miles. Occasionally he broke off a bloom and sniffed it, or crushed a snip of herb to release its aroma. He dug a small notebook from the backpack and made notes and sketches of plants he recognized, and others he didn't.

In a vast plain of white flowers he shrugged off the pack and lay down and stretched. Clouds passed above, none capable of making rain. The sun shone, but gave him no clue of the time. It had hung the same distance above the horizon all the while he'd been there. Chum had heard of the land of the midnight sun, where the sun shone all day long, like it was a tall tale or something. *Guess it's real and that's where I am. Wonder if it's midnight?* He checked his watch. *Huh.* The time was half past a freckle. He only had a bare wrist. Must have dropped the watch when he grappled with Nikki while they were flying. Probably lying in a forest somewhere, ticking away until the battery shuts down. *Maybe someone will go deep into the woods to hunt, and will find the watch, and wonder how the heck it got there. Hahaha.*

He got to his feet, shrugged into the pack, and resumed his trek, always moving toward the mountains. The land changed and became lumpy, like it hid sleeping prehistoric creatures beneath. Soil texture loosened up. Some hollows between humps were boggy, squishy with water where Charlie-Chum stepped. He topped a hillock and stared at the new sight: a land of hills and ponds, some no bigger than a kid's wading pool, some almost large enough to be called lakes. Bushes and thick grasses rimmed the ponds, drinking up water. Chum's energy flared as he jogged down to explore the land of ponds.

The presence of fresh water prodded his thirst, which he'd ignored until now. His dad had trained him in wilderness survival. If you were hungry or thirsty, you couldn't let that fill your mind. Hunger and thirst worked on you like an evil spirit. It drew down your energy and broke your focus on surviving. At the edge of a lake, Charlie-Chum pulled a collapsible jug from the pack and submerged it in fresh, cool water. He dropped in a couple of water-purification tablets, then killed his thirst with long swallows. Nikki had the canteen, and he had also given her a couple of energy bars when they set out on this expedition, so she should be okay. As he thought of Nikki, he heard her voice. He popped up his head and looked around.

"Hey, Charlie-Chum!" Here she came, riding on Belinda, waving her hand like a flag. When she saw him, Nikki jumped off the polar bear and jogged over. Belinda took her time, walking like a slow country-and-western song, swinging her head side to side with the beat.

"What the heck are you doing way over here? We might have lost you." Nikki looked annoyed.

"No, you wouldn't. If you were really worried, you'd fly around and find me. But I bet Belinda caught my stinky human smell. The wind's running from the mountains to the sea. I was upwind of you."

"Smarty. So, how about these ponds? With so much water, I bet there's bear food in this country."

"I hope there's human food, too. Speaking of which, I've been thinking about our situation, with only one pack and all. It's a big problem, but I think we can manage."

"How?"

"The worst thing is food supply. There's enough for one person for two months in this pack. So, each day we've got half rations. We'll bring it to full rations by foraging and trapping and fishing—or else listen to our stomachs grumble."

Nikki responded with a nod. "Good. We can do this."

"I'll manage rations, and you pay attention to bears. Deal?" Charlie-Chum was troubled by Nikki's quiet. He wanted her normal, bouncy self.

"Sure," she said.

Belinda nuzzled Nikki like a giant friendly dog, and Nikki got the message. "Belinda wants to catch up with the others." She mounted the bear. "Come on up, Charlie-Chum."

"Naw. I get motion sick riding a bear. I'll stay on my own two feet and walk alongside you guys."

Belinda followed her nose, literally, tracking the rest of the posse by scent, and found them hanging around atop a two-hundred-foot mound that provided views into brown bear territory. Nikki and Charlie-Chum watched a dozen bears digging, stripping, nosing, and nibbling morsels of food.

"I checked out these guys before we left," Nikki thought aloud. "They're brown bears, same as grizzlies. But these are smaller than usual, because there's not so much food here on the tundra. They're called barren-ground brown bears. I have to admit, tundra food's sure not going to be as satisfying for the polar bears as eating a nice, fat seal."

"Same for us, in a way," Charlie-Chum said. We're going to be eating little bits of stuff, too, or else be on half rations. We're going to have to learn from the brown bears how to eat from this barren ground." He scuffed the stony ground to make the point.

"Windy," Nikki called. She rolled back from the ridge and huddled with her friend. "This place looks like a desert. Whatever can the polar bears live on? I thought there would be lots of bear food where we were leading them." Nikki's satiny eyebrows lifted and her forehead wrinkled.

"No worries, Friend," Windy said. "This tundra hides hundreds and hundreds of kinds of plants, and plenty of small animals. Sure, the polar bears won't feel fat and full as with a meal of seals. And any little ones born here will be smaller as adults. That just means they're adapting to eating off the land, instead of off the ice. There's really no choice for them. You see?" Nikki nodded.

"Besides," added Windy, "I'm certain the brown bears will amble the polar bears up the mountain and into the forest. There's different food up there. Tons of berries. There's nothing happier than a bear in a berry bush."

Feeling better, Nikki scrambled back to the ridge. The polar bears were talking.

"They look small," said one.

"They're not all the same color," said another.

"Red brown, nut brown, golden brown. Some even yellow-white—like a dirty polar bear."

"What are they doing, digging in the dirt?" Belinda asked.

"They're scratching out food. Ground squirrels, roots, grubs, stuff like that," Nikki said. This made her think of TV reality shows, where ordinary people got dumped in the wild some-where. They ended up eating bugs and furry little animals. *Too gross!* But brown bears loved their food.

Nikki listened to the polar bears around her. They looked uneasy, shifting from foot to foot, and they muttered. She crept got close to Ssorog and listened.

"What a stupid move, to come out here. I'll never eat what-ever it is those runty brown bears are getting from stones and weeds. Where's the meat?" he growled to himself.

Now that Nikki had wandered off, Belinda worried, too. "I don't see how we can become fat and healthy in this place. But maybe the brown bears have the secret and will teach us."

Ticcar was concerned, as well. "My leadership has brought us to this? I don't see how my bears can thrive here. I shall be ashamed."

But Windy bucked him up. "Chief, stay strong. I've spent time with these bears, and they know things about this land, and where to find food—good food—that polar bears don't. That's the whole point. Have courage. See the biggest boar, on the near edge of that lake? He's Wenobri, the chief. He's waiting for you."

Nikki reappeared, next to Charlie-Chum. "They're all worry-ing that this expedition is a failure before it starts, because there's nothing here a polar bear can eat and get fat on. But I'm with Windy. He told the chief to stay strong. Let's see what happens."

That was a pep talk for Chum. Nikki had reservations. She frowned as she surveyed their summer home. It was the same flat land they'd been traveling through, wind scrubbed and cold-cured. Plants and little creatures apparently were there for the eating, but she'd never have picked this place for their experiment. *The ponds and lakes were encouraging. They probably held fish,* she thought. And barely visible from the height of this hill, a pale river ran, zinging and sparkling, to the sea.

But in her mind's eye, before they started out, Nikki had anticipated a green, grass-softened valley. She'd looked for bushes, trees, hills, and cave-holding mountains as well. The drained and empty land she saw now put a cold weight in her stomach, as if she'd swallowed a stone. Had she and Windy done a terrible wrong to the Polar Bears? *What if the bears starved on this tundra at the edge of the mountains, instead of starving on the tundra at the edge of the sea?*

She and Charlie-Chum sank to the ground, a safe distance away from the muttering polar bears, to see what would happen.

"All right," said Ticcar. "I've seen enough. Let's take the plunge. NO FIGHTING," he warned, looking at Ssorog. "We'll stay calm and use our smarts. We want these bears to respect us."

Ticcar stood tall on the ridge and showed himself. This caused the brown bears to stop foraging and train their eyes on the newcomers. Ticcar lumbered down the slope. The others followed. Windy flew over to Wenobri and waited for the polar bears to cross the valley. As for Nikki, she moved along at Ticcar's side.

Chief Ticcar padded down the hill. Softly, softly Ticcar continued, toward Wenobri, who sat unconcerned on his haunches, nibbling morsels from a bush. Ticcar closed the distance between them to ten yards. Wenobri allowed his grazing to be interrupted by the stranger. He stood on all fours and stared as the new bear kept coming. There's a law among bears that one doesn't invade another's space without expecting trouble. This was trouble.

Ticcar, the troublemaker, rushed the final yards and tackled Wenobri. The two rose on their hind legs and grappled like wrestlers. Muzzles gaped and teeth slashed, horrendous bellows boiled up from their guts. Blood ran from a bite on Ticcar's muzzle and stained his white fur. He bit the flesh above Wenobri's eye and dripping blood made it hard for Wenobri to see. Ticcar threw his opponent to the ground. Over and over they rolled, roaring to shake the earth, striking with tooth and claw.

Before any serious damage was done, Ticcar regained his feet and padded away. He was bigger and stronger than the brown bear and should have won, but the fight was symbolic. By declaring himself to be the loser, Ticcar submitted to Wenobri as bear chief in this territory. Now Ticcar's polar bear posse could live in peace among Wenobri's brown bears. Learning could begin.

Nikki and Charlie-Chum watched the polar bears leave the hill and meet their chief. Ticcar was hobbled by a sore shoulder and bloodied from a few inconsequential cuts, which would heal on their own.

There was enough food this season, more than the brown bears could eat. So they didn't care if new bears joined them. As long as those guys didn't make trouble. Respect. Respect was what the brown bears required.

As the polar bear pioneers approached the brown bears, there came a critical moment. *Would the two groups meet in peace? Or would there be a big, beary brawl?* Nikki clutched Ticcar's fur and held her breath.

The meeting turned out to be a non-event. The bears retained a respectful distance and mutually concluded the other bears were okay. There was no need for formal introduction, as Windy already had worked that out. Nikki watched in admiration as Wenobri set the tone. First catching Ticcar's eye, to be sure he was observing, Wenobri put his nose to the ground, found something tasty, dug it out with his claws, and popped it into his mouth. Ticcar imitated him. Soon he, too, was successfully putting together a belly-soothing meal.

Nikki crouched on the ground and watched. Wenobri's six-inch claws were more effective tools for digging than Ticcar's shorter ones, but Ticcar possessed a keener sense of smell. Both were intelligent. Wenobri taught well, and Ticcar had early success in reading the soil and plants. From Wenobri he also learned to experiment. If he dug up a different bug or root, he'd sample it, to see if it were tasty. When one of them flushed out a ground squirrel or other little rodent, that was a big deal. A morsel of meat! As this went on, other brown bears and polar bears fanned out to explore. It became a scene of quiet diligence, searching for and swallowing a good meal, though it took all day and the polar bears never gained that satisfying feeling of a full stomach.

CHAPTER THIRTEEN

"LET'S GET SOME DISTANCE BETWEEN us and all these bears," said Charlie-Chum. "Watching that display of aggression convinces me that our camp should be somewhere they aren't. How about over toward that river in the distance?"

"Fine with me," Nikki said.

"Windy! Oh, Windy!" she called, turning in a circle and searching the sky.

"What're you doing that for?"

"I'm going to ask Windy to be our guard, all the time. Especially when we sleep."

"Excellent. Windy's a super guy. He saved me from falling to my death, you remember."

Windy came, and it was arranged.

"With pleasure, my dear," he said.

The two hiked on, until they fetched up at the river. At a bend, fast water had undercut the bank, sculpting a bluff. Here

Charlie-Chum set up the tent. They weren't sure what to do with their supply of food: bears would love to eat it. Camping at home, they'd hang it from a rope tied to a tree limb. Bears can climb trees, but usually they can't figure out the rope.

"No trees here, Chum, to hang our food from."

"Actually, there are trees here, I found out, only they're miniature. I found a willow and it was only three inches high! Aspen, birches, trees like that grow like bushes, not trees. I guess winter storms keep them small."

"What if we bury the food?"

"The bears'll dig it up."

"Okay, let's put a big rock on top."

"Bears can move a rock if they want to."

"Well, maybe they'll have more interesting things to do. It's the best option.

So they cached their food in a hole in the ground, the permafrost, which was thawed for the top several feet. A folding camp shovel did the trick. Then they buckled their sturdy leather belts together to make a long strap. They looped the strap around a hunk of a rock, and leaned into the load like a couple of draft horses. "One-two-three-PULL," Charlie-Chum called, and they lugged it over to secure the cache.

"Okay, I'm off to dig us a latrine," Charlie-Chum volunteered.

"Be sure to choose a nice shrubby spot, so the latrine's private!" Nikki called after him. This was extremely important, but he was a boy and might not think so. She always closed the bathroom door, and out here there was no such thing. Sighing, she made the bed. The tent was barely big enough for two people, and the sleeping bag was for one. She laid out the foam sleeping pad crosswise. That way she and Chum could have the pad cushion the areas from hip to shoulder. She unzipped the down sleeping bag, spread it open, and shook it out like a blanket. That would have to do. Nikki wasn't exactly embarrassed to share a bed with Charlie-Chum—they were such good friends, and cousins, after all. But he was a boy, so the situation was a little strange. They'd be sleeping in their clothes, anyway, because there never was any room in a backpack for pajamas.

Nikki had just placed the camp stove and fuel in a corner at the foot of the tent when Charlie-Chum returned from digging.

"Got a nice spot for us. I think your modesty will be satisfied."

"Thanks, Chum. Come see what I've done."

He poked his head into the tent. "Not bad. You know, if we sleep close together like that, we'll keep each other warm with body heat." He saw a dubious look cross Nikki's face. "Of course, if you want we can sleep head to foot. You know, your head and my feet at one end ..."

"Eeew, I'd any day rather have your face next to my head than your feet. Do you know how gross your feet are?"

Charlie-Chum backed out of the tent. "You hurt my feelings. I have nice feet."

"Whatever. We'll both have our heads at the same end, thank you very much."

"One good thing. We don't have to worry about lanterns. Looks like we have plenty of long summer daylight. It might be hard to sleep, actually, without the dark night."

But they were exhausted, and nodded off instantly.

The next morning, Charlie-Chum was off somewhere, but Nikki wasn't worried—she knew Windy would keep an eye on him. Meanwhile, Nikki was glad she had persuaded Chum to pack sketching materials. She pulled out a sketchbook and used a fine black pen to draw the rare scenes around her: Polar bears learning new feeding skills from brown bears. *Could it be that Windy's and her hope of saving the polar bears was coming true? Could the polar bears change and live?* Colored pencils brought life to her sketches. Nikki dated each one, and wrote notes in the white margins. With arrows she pointed to bears she knew by name: Ticcar, Belinda, Ssorog, Wenobri. Sometimes, for fun, Nikki added balloons of bear-thought.

Belinda: "That Wenobri is handsome." Nikki drew long eyelashes on her, the better to flutter at her heartthrob.

Wenobri: "Belinda's a good mother. Look how she takes care of that human cub."

Ssorog: "Bleaaath. Plants and roots. Grass and flowers. Little animals worth only a toothful. Where's the real meat?"

Ticcar: Sigh of relief. "Just eat and rest now. All is good."

Around dinner time, by her watch, Chum returned with tales of what he'd discovered and a bowl brimming with berries. His big find was a collection of herbs he laid out on rocks to dry in the sun, then he would label them, tuck them into baggies, and take them home. He'd ask Grandma about the ones he didn't recognize.

"Say, Nikki, I saw bears digging for clams. Let's climb down to the river and get some for our dinner!" They did that, then built a fire on the river bank and simmered the clams in fresh river water with aromatic herbs to make a tasty broth. Berries and half a granola bar each were for dessert.

They had a solar charger for Chum's cell phone. Even without wireless connection in this wilderness, they had books to read on the phone. First was Jack London's *The Call of the Wild*. Lounging around the coals of their campfire, Nikki read aloud. The main character was an incredibly brave sled dog named Buck, in Alaska and Canada for the gold rush of the 1890s. He started out as a normal pet, who was stolen from a backyard in California. He was big and strong, and became sort of a prisoner as he was transferred from one owner to another, some of whom treated him brutally. Finally, the dog's last owners were killed and Buck answered the call of the wild, trotting off into the forest to join a pack of wolves. The story was packed with action and danger, emotion and suspense. Soon enough the two tired, stirred out the fire, and climbed back to the tent, where the shady interior made it possible to sleep despite the sunlight, once they got used to it.

"Night, Charlie-Chum," Nikki mumbled.

"Night, Nikki," he said.

Time passed. Nikki lost track of the days. She followed one bear or another and sketched whatever they were doing: Playing, eating, sleeping. The brown bears were as interesting characters as the polar bears. They were willing to have her around, since she spoke Bear. Once or twice a bear took a swipe at Nikki, but she just flew a distance away, and got out of reach. After that, the bears seemed to think the human cub was too much trouble to mess with. Often Nikki accompanied Windy as he flew in search of quarry. Frequently she and Belinda lazed around together, passing the time of day. Belinda loved to have Nikki rub her tummy. Nikki's naturalist's soul was filling up.

CHAPTER FOURTEEN

ONE DAY, GLIDING THROUGH THE air on her front and back, executing slow rolls and loops, Nikki spotted a polar bear coming along the trail they had made from Polar Bear Land. The bear was resting now, but would soon come over the ridge. Nikki located Ticcar and plunged down to him. Windy was with her.

"Ticcar, Ticcar," Nikki said. "A bear is coming here from Polar Bear Land. She's resting, just the other side of the ridge. Look! Here she comes now."

They watched, at first with curiosity, then with dismay, as the polar bear swayed toward them. This bear's fur hung on her as if it were a hand-me-down from a bigger sister. Ticcar, Nikki, and Windy hurried to meet her. The newcomer slumped to the ground as if she would never move again. Nikki patted her shoulder and cooed.

"Hello, my poor Ellen," said Ticcar, touching noses. "You're worn out, dear thing. You rest and we'll get you some food. Albert!" Ticcar barked over his shoulder. A young male polar bear trotted over. "Listen, Ellen here needs to eat. She hasn't much time, but we can save her. Run over and get a bunch of youngsters to bring food.

"Ellen," Ticcar continued, "why did you come? Is everyone in as bad shape as you are? Tell us, tell us what terrible news you bring."

"There's hardly anything. To eat back there," Ellen gasped as she spoke. "Polar Bear Land. Walking starvation." More ragged breaths. "No life for me there. Please let me stay. With you." She touched his arm. "Ticcar."

"Of course you must stay," Ticcar said. "You will recover and be your wonderful self again." Ticcar fell silent, but continued to study Ellen. Something else bothered him. "Ellen, I'm thinking you have something else to tell. What is it?"

"Rollo is dead."

Ticcar sat down and slumped his large bullet head and neck between his knees. He was the ultimate picture of grief.

"How?" he asked.

"Nothing special. The new norm," said Ellen. "You saw how thin. Didn't you notice? Cough at council?"

"This is all my fault," Ticcar moaned. "I'm the one who made Rollo stay behind. He is—was—the soul of loyalty. Rollo always anticipated my needs and filled them. Never a thought for his own welfare. I wanted him to stay in Polar Bear Land to take care of business. What business? How idiotic. The only business now is saving life. I wouldn't let Rollo come with us and live." Ticcar shook his head side to side in remorse.

By now Ellen was munching on green sedges and roots, nibbling on quantities of moths and bugs, swallowing several voles whole. Already she was sitting up.

"Ticcar," Ellen said, beginning to feel blood coursing through her. "Another terrible thing happened back home."

"Oh, no!" Nikki said in a strained voice.

"Tell us, Ellen," said Ticcar.

"Three of our young, brash boars went where the humans live. Since there were three, they made each other bold. They picked through piles on the edge of human land. Sharp things cut their feet, but they also picked out food. Strange food, but nourishing. Then they made their big mistakes. The youngsters sniffed around the human dens. They put their noses through openings. They walked into a den, and of course they could smell where the food was. The boars dug and scraped and tore and had an orgy of gluttony. But one boar sensed danger. Teha, remember him? One of the youngsters. He got out of there and hid."

"It was a good thing, too. As Teha watched, a loud machine came up the trail, twice as fast as the fastest polar bear can run. He saw human boars with fire sticks run into the den. He heard fire stick barks. Next, machines came down from the sky. Things like bird wings swung around on top of the sky machines. More human boars ran from the sky machines to the den."

"No sight or sound came from the two polar bears inside. But soon each one came out, dragged by the humans. The bears were tangled in some kind of seaweed. Humans fastened each tangled bear to the bottom of a sky machine. The sight of polar bears treated like that was humiliating. It was terrifying, Teha told us."

"Something even worse happened next. The sky machines' wings moved fast and faster, loud and louder. The machines rose into the sky. Our boars dangled from the bottom like a berry from a branch, ready to fall. And, oh Ticcar, listen to this!"

Ticcar was trying to keep control of himself, to speak with a level tone. "What, Ellen. Tell us."

"Those sky machines went higher and higher, and our bears became smaller and smaller. Teha said they were curled up and as small, small, small as a helpless newborn polar bear cub. And then they just vanished."

"Teha galloped home with the news. Oh, Ticcar, what happened to our boars? Did they grow backward, from adult to tiny cub to nothing? It's too horrible." By now Ellen was as hysterical with grief as her weakened condition would allow.

Nikki explained. "Ellen, you'll be surprised. There's a happy end to that story. Fire sticks put the boars to sleep. The sky machines carried them gently to some place far away, in a different part of Polar Bear Land where there are no humans. The tangles will be removed, the humans will leave in their sky machines, and the bears will wake up. They'll be confused, but those two will just start over as normal polar bears."

"But," Nikki said in a very firm voice, "don't think all human fire sticks are harmless. Most kill. And some humans hunt for polar bears to kill. The important thing is never, ever to go where humans live. You must expect that human places are death to polar bears."

Ticcar turned toward the path where Ellen had emerged. "I am going to return to Polar Bear Land. The situation here seems pretty stable, with polar bears and brown bears coexisting peacefully. On the other hand, I must go where I am most needed, and that is back where my polar bears are in trouble. I'll return when I can."

It had become Nikki's habit each day to tag along with one bear or another, or a few. This day, Nikki set her sights on Ssorog. She thought he had become too confident about his skills and about his rank among the bears in this new place. Ssorog had always contended with Ticcar. Now that Ticcar had gone home, Nikki sensed that Ssorog would soon contend with Wenobri. Nikki hated this possibility. She and her friends were attempting a life-giving experiment to save polar bears. Nikki was desperate for Ssorog not to ruin everything by starting a battle. It could even become a war between the polar bears and the brown bears. Her brain curdled at the thought.

"Followme," Nikki said, "I'm worried about Ssorog. I'm not sure what his plan is, but I think he will choose to fight Wenobri. Then what can we do?"

"Let's see what he does this day. Maybe there will be a clue."

Ssorog was being independent as usual. Nikki had crept behind him for some miles, tucking herself into plots of shrubbery and staying into low places in the hilly ground. She was careful to stay downwind of him, so he wouldn't catch her scent. Nikki didn't think she smelled, but to a bear she reeked. As for smell, Ssorog was after something. He kept stopping, standing and reaching his nose up to catch the breeze, which was redolent of something. Nikki couldn't imagine what. To get a better view, she slithered up a small rise. Down on a grassy level, Nikki saw Ssorog's discovery: a small herd of musk oxen.

Nikki was stunned. This was a breed of megafauna that still survived, the one contradiction to the last Ice Age's ending. A musk ox is an Ice Age creature. Nikki's head swam. This was like time travel.

Ssorog wasn't used to crafty hunting. Back home on the ice, a polar bear just waited patiently—for hours—until a seal surfaced from its realm below the ice. Then, quick as the flip of a fish tail, the bear snapped up the seal. Nikki wondered if Ssorog had any idea how to take down a musk ox.

From her hiding place, Nikki could see and hear every detail. She grasped Followme and stroked him anxiously as she watched in fascination. Ssorog crept toward his prey until he got within striking range. But he had no chance to gallop and surprise, because the meadow was open and he was huge and obvious. The oxen saw their one-ton enemy long before he got close. Somehow they communicated and the herd formed a defensive position, a circle with shaggy brown heads pointing outward. Calves stuck to their mothers or sheltered inside the circle. Grassy smells arose from the trampled ground, and flowers broke from their stems.

Prepared, the musk oxen waited in their living fortress. Ssorog stopped short at the sight of this apparent twenty-headed creature. Together they were fearsome. Each ox presented a monstrous head, crowned by lethal curved horns, backed up by a hump of muscle over the shoulders. Nikki thought these buffalo-like animals could be a match for Ssorog. They were about the same height at the shoulder. Of course, he had teeth and claws, but the musk oxen had horns and hooves.

Ssorog had no thought this would be an equal match. He was a giant compared to these unfortunate lumps. Only a few lengths away now, Ssorog paced. He was excited by this fight. This was living, as far as he was concerned. Fight. Live or die. Eat or be eaten. This day he would live and eat.

"AAAAAARRRRGggggghhhhhh!" Ssorog bellowed and rose on his hind legs, towering over the musk oxen.

A bull musk ox stepped out of the ring and confronted Ssorog. He bellowed with a sound so sonorous and deep it seemed to rise from the earth beneath his hooves.

"BBBBBBOOOOOOUUUUUAAAAaaggggghhhhhh!"

Ssorog growled and showed his teeth.

The bull snorted and swung his horns. Meanwhile the rest of the herd scattered and disappeared. Only the two contestants remained on the field of battle.

Ssorog moved left to get the bull's flank. The bull countered.

Dust puffed under the bull's stamping hooves.

Ssorog backed away for a fresh start. The bull charged and knocked him in the snout with the shield-like boss between his horns. Caught off balance, Ssorog rolled over. That boss was hard as iron. Ssorog had never felt anything like it. He shook his head to clear the blackness obscuring his eyesight. At the same time, Ssorog scrambled back to his feet and faced his attacker. How humiliating for a polar bear—not just any polar bear, but the strongest polar bear ever—to be downed by a stupid musk ox.

Wasting no time, Ssorog roared and lunged at the bull's snout. Ssorog opened his knife-toothed mouth wide and clamped down hard. The bull bellowed and tried to shake Ssorog off, but Ssorog would not yield. With his breath cut off and blood draining down his throat, the bull was weakening.

Ssorog released his grip, but the bull was not done yet. With a mighty toss of his head, the bull sliced at Ssorog and scored a vicious wound in Ssorog's neck. Both fighters were now blooded. The wound on Ssorog's neck was well-placed, and blood gushed onto his white fur.

Now Ssorog saw his opportunity. While the musk ox's face was momentarily angled away, Ssorog attacked. Teeth in the bull's shoulder, arms and claws trapping his opponent's body, Ssorog used his superior weight to down the bull. A ferocious bite to the jugular, and in minutes the fight was over. Ssorog was the victor. He was somewhat the worse for wear, but his neck wound was clotting already.

Now, the feast.

Nikki was overcome by admiration for Ssorog. The polar bears needed an individual that strong, that courageous, that inured to risk. If only he could use those characteristics well, not destructively. Nikki noticed a bunch of teenage bears, brown and polar, hiding behind a clump of willows. *I suppose they saw the whole thing,* Nikki thought. Just as well: that was an unforgettable lesson in hunting Ssorog just delivered.

Nikki watched Ssorog eat until he could eat no more. The giant lay down a few paces away to sleep it off. He allowed the youngsters to creep up and eat, now that he was done. Of course, he gave them a few cuffs and growls to make them remember who was boss, then returned to his nap.

CHAPTER FIFTEEN

SSOROG'S HUNTING PROWESS BECAME LEGEND
in the bear camp. It was not often that any bear achieved solo
victory over a musk ox. Since this was Ssorog's first encounter
with the ice-age monster, the polar bear became recognized
for his innate strategic sense, fighting skill, and brute strength.
Nikki noticed that young boars followed him and showed off,
each hoping to attract the hero's attention and become his favorite. Ssorog allowed a sort of tribe to gather around him. In fact,
he encouraged it and his tribe grew. These bears went where
Ssorog went and did what Ssorog said.

Nikki confided her troubled thoughts to Followme. "I'm just
sure that, with his new hunting reputation, and all of the young
bears tagging after him, Ssorog will use his growing power for
no good."

"You are right to be troubled," the little polar bear replied.
"In my opinion Ssorog is is preparing for his ultimate goal: He

wants to unseat Wenobri as leader in this place. Since Ticcar is back in Polar Bear Land, Wenobri is the only bear in his way."

Pondering this, Nikki wandered on foot and in flight, trying to find Belinda. She hadn't seen her for a few days, and Nikki wanted to discuss the Ssorog problem. Belinda might have wisdom to offer. Having traipsed a good distance, she finally spotted Belinda in a tidy meadow. But at the sight, Nikki stopped. She sat on a lichen-crusted boulder some distance away and observed, with respect and delight. She had come upon Belinda and Wenobri in love. It was the sweetest picture. Brown and white, white and brown, cuddling in fresh green grass. What Nikki saw was like the princess and prince joining two kingdoms, allowing everyone to live happily ever after.

Nikki slipped away, her heart light. With Belinda and Wenobri together, Ssorog would never be able to wreck the peaceful experiment of polar bears and brown bears sharing territory and living well. She met up with Charlie-Chum, thinking about dinner.

"Hey, Chum, what's new?"

"I found a new bed of clams, and brought a mess of them back in my hat for dinner."

"I sure am hungry for some good bread, to sop up the clam juices," sighed Nikki.

"Yeah, but we can add some instant rice to the broth and that'll be almost as good."

Over dinner, Nikki reminded Chum of Ssorog's battle with the musk ox, and the tribe of young bears being attracted to his leadership. "Then today I saw Belinda and Wenobri together, and I'm not worried anymore about Ssorog toppling Wenobri from power. Sure, he'll always be a bad boy. He will always be making trouble. But now I'm pretty sure—with Belinda and Wenobri joining the polar bears and the brown bears—Ssorog can only be an annoyance rather than a threat to the power couple. This is a very good day, Chum!"

"I want to have an exciting day like yours, Nikki," Chum protested. "So I found a bed of clams, big deal."

"It is a big deal, because now we can eat," said Nikki. "Besides, I have a hunch that Ssorog is going to try—even though I think he will fail—to upset the power around here. And he'll do it soon, while he is riding high on his hunting triumph. If he does, there will be excitement enough for both of us."

After dinner, Nikki sketched from memory Belinda and Wenobri, sitting side by side, leaning up against each other. She loved the way bears slumped when they sat, like bean-bag toys. Nikki thought she would make a pair of bean-bag bears, a little Belinda and a little Wenobri, when she got back home. Velvet for bodies, small black buttons for eyes. She would make mouths that opened. A blue tongue for Belinda and a red one for Wenobri. She'd have to think a bit more about teeth and claws. She wanted them to look sharp, but not be sharp.

While she was deep inside her mind's eye, imagining these things, a low, growly hum startled her. The images in her head dissolved and she saw once more the shrubby meadow of their campsite. Nikki and Charlie-Chum turned toward the sound and saw that Belinda had come to visit.

"Nikki, my dear cub! And Chum, my little boar!" exclaimed Belinda.

Nikki set her sketching materials neatly on the grass and ran to give Belinda a hug and snuggle. Belinda lay down and rolled onto her back. Nikki climbed up and lay face down on Belinda, stretching full length on the polar bear's soft tummy. Nikki stilled and could hear Belinda's heart beating. *Bears aren't much different from us,* Nikki thought, listening to the reassuring ta-DUM ta-DUM ta-DUM. Many times when she was younger, she had stretched out this same way on her mama's tummy and listened to her heart. Ta-DUM ta-DUM ta-DUM. In the soft breeze and warm sun of the arctic evening, bear and girl closed their eyes and drifted into a nap, forgetting about poor Chum, who had been writing poems about his day. He sighed, and returned to his writing. Belinda and Nikki had a special thing going on, and that was that.

But Nikki's nap was short. This time, a different sound startled her and Belinda, too. This was like the sound of her mama shaking the crumbs off a tablecloth out in the back yard. Snap-snap-rustle-flap. Both scrambled up, alert. But their defenses fell away when they saw it was Windy, settling on a shrub.

"Hey, Windy," Nikki greeted him. She walked over and smoothed the feathers of his back. Windy always kept his same fierce face, but she knew he liked the petting, because he never squirmed under her touch. "Looks like we have the executive committee here. Whatever needs to be done, we can do it."

"What needs to be done, Nikki?" asked the bear and raptor at the same time.

Nikki explained the fears Followme and she had about Ssorog preparing for a power upset.

Windy spoke. "I've been keeping an eye on the big boy, and listening to the bears. Obviously, he's swaggering around boasting about his musk ox kill, and that's impressing a lot of bears. Many think Ssorog can do no wrong. They'll back him in a blink. If he's a successful hunter, he must be a successful leader. Power speaks."

Nikki's eyes slitted in worried thought. "This sounds awful," she said. "We can't let Ssorog wreck the experiment. The deal was for peace. As long as Ticcar was here to work with Wenobri, the bears had it made. Just look how full the starving polar bears are now, because they've watched and learned from brown bears. If Ssorog makes this new polar bear–brown bear thing all about him and who his guys are and all that, then we'll have bloody struggle instead of good peace."

"Besides, we need nice healthy bears to produce healthy babies." Nikki cut her eyes over to Belinda, wondering if she'd pick up the lead.

"Listen, you two. I have good, good news!" Her leathery lips curved into a smile. "Today Wenobri and I fell in love and I know, I just know, we will have beautiful cubs some day. They will be healthy and smart and strong. Not to mention adorable."

Then in a fierce tone she added, "Wenobri and I won't allow any bear to interfere with this new way of life. We have a new generation to come and we will protect it."

Excited, Nikki clapped her hands. "I'm so happy for you. And with you and Wenobri leading the good life, Ssorog's power grab will fade like fog."

"We hope so," said Windy. "Congratulations, Belinda my friend, on your good news. But good news can have the strange effect of attracting bad reactions. Let's not drop our guard."

"Oh, Windy, you're always so serious," teased Nikki with a playful poke at his breast. "Haven't you ever done something silly, just for fun?"

"I don't even know what you mean. Silliness. That must be a human thing. Peregrines don't do it."

"Well, I'll do it right now. I'm silly with happiness for Belinda and Wenobri ... and all the bears ... and everything good ... that's happening in this ... beautiful place." Nikki was turning silly cartwheels around her friends. She came back rosy-cheeked and panting, and flopped down. "Whew. That was fun."

"Now you," Belinda said, turning to the grinning Nikki, "Listen to me. Even when my new cubs are born, you will always be my cub, too. You are my sweet silly young sow, who was dead in the sea but born to me when I brought you out."

Nikki felt treasured, although she had never been called a sow before. She also felt tired. Having shared her worries with Windy and Belinda, a burden of concern lifted from her shoulders. Letting down, Nikki didn't bother to cover up a huge yawn. She was forgetting her manners up here. Yawns are catching, and Belinda caught it, stretching open her mouth and curling out her tongue and drawing her lips back from her teeth. Nikki didn't know whether to laugh or cringe at the sight. She did know that it was time for bed.

"Okay, you guys, I'm going to sleep. See you in the morning." *Morning? Well, in a manner of speaking. The sun would just be in a different part of the sky.* She put away the sketching materials and quickly brushed her teeth. She crept into the tent, where Chum had beat her to it, sleeping with his head buried in his arm to keep out the daylight. Then she dreamed of peace forever between the polar bears and the brown bears.

The next day when Nikki awoke she crawled out of the tent and stretched in the fresh air, one hand high to the sky, the other hand high to the sky. She shook a leg or two, bent from the waist and swung like a rag doll, then walked her hands ahead on the gritty ground till she was flat as a plank. She bounced up and danced to music in her head. Nikki pulled on fresh shorts and a T-shirt that she'd washed in a pool and dried overnight on a rock, and jogged barefoot over to the river. Wherever the bears had wandered over the summer, they were never far from the river, and this suited Nikki fine. Every day she and Chum dipped in the cold water. Shorts and T-shirts were their swimming costumes. They splashed and laughed and tingled and felt alive. Veins in their wrists tightened out of sight, protecting warm blood from the chill.

Dressed and idling along the river bank, drying out, Nikki searched head down for interesting stones. Lately she liked to draw on any smooth rock, using it like a blackboard. She scratched the rock with softer stones of various colors. It was like drawing with chalk. She drew images of home. There was the house. An arrow pointed to her room, and the white pine woods stood to the side. There was Mama, with Daddy next to her.

Always there were several bears at the river, turning over stones, probing vegetation at the water's edge. Usually the search was rewarded by snails or bugs. But today Nikki noticed increased bear activity at the river. Many stood completely in the water. Eyes were fixed on fresh riffles and still pools and ropey currents. The bears looked like they were waiting for something.

Nikki was intrigued. She fastened her eyes on the bears and shouted with surprise when one of them put in a paw and pulled out a big fish. All over the river this began happening. It was salmon time. The fatty fish were swimming from the sea up the river to spawn. By some mysterious knowledge, the fish were returning to the very same river where they had hatched. Once there, females released orange, jelly-like eggs. At the same time, males ejected a cloud of sperm. With water as the mating medium, the eggs were fertilized and new life began.

In the coming days, salmon crowded the river and made the surface roll as if it boiled. Bears were everywhere, grabbing and tearing into fish without pause. The polar bears were thrilled to have full stomachs, though it took them a while to learn the technique. At the beginning, numerous fish got away from them. Many bears took their catches to a rock or riverbank to eat, but some just bit and shredded and swallowed in midstream. Seagulls and bald eagles nipped up the scraps. Careful not to get in the way, Nikki and Charlie-Chum joined in. Chum used a stuff sack from the backpack to catch a fish. He scaled and gutted the salmon using a hunting knife, speared it on a green willow branch, and roasted it over coals. The meat was succulent and perfect.

Chum and Nikki loved this rich food. Fingers picked juicy fish and charred skin from the bone. Lips sucked each finger clean. Fire-hot stones dropped in two mugs heated water for fresh mint tea. The pair shared the last chocolate brownie bar. *Chocolate!* Nikki really missed chocolate. *Chocolate ice cream, chocolate chip cookies, chocolate cake, chocolate-covered caramels, chocolate milkshakes, chocolate fudge sauce that became chewy colliding with cold scoops of vanilla ice cream in a dish. Oh, man!* Nikki wished for that and began to long for home. She breathed in the luxurious aroma of the brownie and ate only one bite, chewing slowly. The rest she stowed in the pocket of her shorts, to nibble afterwards.

A few days later when Nikki and Chum joined bears at the salmon run, there was a different feel about it. Nikki sniffed the air, studied the water, checked out the salmon, and squinted at sun and clouds. *Nothing unusual at all.* But the bears ... the bears were tense. This made Nikki tense. What did they know that she didn't? In this place, Nikki always wanted to see a paradise, abundance and safety for all. But Followme warned her to pay attention.

"Keep a constant guard against the bears, my dear. After all, they are savage animals first and your friends only as long as they feel like it." Especially under Ssorog's spell, bear behavior could turn nasty in a flash. She could become their dinner. She trusted Belinda though, who, after all, had saved her life. She wanted Belinda.

But Belinda wasn't in sight, and Nikki didn't dare search for her among the nervous bears. Better not to blunder into something bad. So Nikki wanted another trusted friend. Cupping hands around her mouth she called out, "Win-dy, Win-dy. Where are you? Oh Win-dy. I need you." Nikki turned in every direction as she called. Would he hear her? Could he tell her what was going on? Nikki clambered up a high rock not far from the riverbank. Waiting for Windy, she lay flat on her stomach, chin on her hands, surveying the bears and the river. She dug a few salted peanuts out of her pocket for energy.

Too much time passed, and still Nikki was alone, with just Followme. "I need to know what Windy sees the bears doing, Followme." She was just about to call for Windy again when he zoomed down into a show-off stoop next to her. Nikki rolled onto her side, head on her hand, and welcomed her friend.

"Oh, Windy, you know I love your stoops. Fastest peregrine in the Arctic, you are. And am I ever glad to see you, buddy."

"What's wrong, my dear?"

"That's what I want you to tell me," she replied in a low voice. "The bears are nervous. You know their normal fishing style. Just plop and flop in the river, and the only thing a bear concentrates on is a good fishing spot. When a salmon comes, zap!"

"Right," Windy agreed.

"But now, the bears are concentrating on each other. I think they expect something to happen. I'm afraid it will be bad. What do you think? Could it be Ssorog?"

CHAPTER SIXTEEN

"LET ME DO SOME RECONNAISSANCE."

"Okay, I'll stay here. I see Wenobri, and I want to keep an eye on him."

Windy's yellow claws scraped the rock as he took off. Nikki watched him fly upriver, banking wide on each side, and disappearing from sight. Soon he returned.

"I think there will be a battle." Windy said.

Nikki gasped. "What do you mean?"

"Here's the recon. You've been watching Wenobri?" Nikki nodded. "He's got prime location, best fishing hole. Notice how the others, brown bears and polar bears, respect his rights as leader. No one is even close to stealing Wenobri's catches."

"Sure, that's normal. Right here there's more salmon than ten times as many bears could handle. No need to crowd Wenobri, or anyone else," said Nikki.

"Until today. Ssorog is just upstream, and those bears know it. He's coming this way. And he's not fishing. He's coming to crowd Wenobri."

Looking into the distance, Nikki saw bears abandon their fishing and run—actually run—out of the water. None wanted part in what was coming, not even Ssorog's rowdy tribe. Clumsy splashes churned the river where the bears had been.

Wenobri hadn't become leader by being stupid. He knew something was up, he read his bears' anxiety. But he would wait until trouble became clear before taking action. So he kept fishing, his eyes wide open. Until bears abandoned the salmon and galloped out of the river. No bear would do that unless frightened. Clearly, trouble was coming. Time to stop fishing. Wenobri waited, four-footed in the river, facing upstream.

And Belinda waited, too. Obscured by boulders and trees, she stayed near the father of her precious cubs-to-be. A sow protecting her cubs, is a fighting force. Belinda would join the battle if needed. Or even if not needed. She was smaller than either of the big males, but just as fierce, perhaps more so. She wanted to hurt and humiliate Ssorog beyond recovery. She wanted him gone. Away. Anywhere but here.

And now trouble appeared just rounding the bend, striding four-footed with careless power along the riverbank. Watching Ssorog close in on Wenobri. Nikki was reminded of old movies, Westerns. She had watched the classic *High Noon* tons of times at home. It was her parents' favorite. The sheriff and the outlaw met in the street, had a gunfight, and only one survived, the good guy. Here Wenobri was the sheriff, and Ssorog was the outlaw.

Nikki watched Ssorog set up his showdown. *Was it her imagination?* Ssorog, now on his hind legs, was doing an aggressive cowboy walk. A bow-legged swagger. Seriously, Nikki almost wouldn't be surprised to see Ssorog wearing a gun belt and pair of six-shooters.

Huge when he arrived in brown bear territory, now Ssorog was even more impressive, heavy with muscle and bulky with fat. He had fed well. Approaching his chosen foe, Ssorog bellowed his battle cry. The sound made Nikki's skin prickle. It struck fear in her, and made the hair rise on the back of her neck. The aggressor now four-footed into the river and came within ten body lengths of Wenobri. One great lunge by each and they would be into it, tooth to tooth, claw to claw. The big brown bear stood fast. Let Ssorog come to him. Wenobri would not flee like a suckling cub. His eyes glittered at Ssorog. Knowledge and power were in those sparks. Wenobri had long known that one day Ssorog would challenge him for leadership. Boss bear of all Arctic bears in this place, Wenobri was ready. Let the fight begin.

Ssorog moved first. He bolted upright and let out a blood-chilling roar. The sound reverberated and seemed to make even the stones shudder. Wenobri reciprocated, standing to full height, not equal, but a fair match. The roars were like drawn swords, intended to put fear into the enemy. But neither contender showed fear.

Then the deadly scramble broke out. Jaws wide open, each went for the other's mouth. It looked like their teeth would lock together. Bites drew blood. Wenobri broke one of Ssorog's huge canine teeth, which then slanted out of his mouth but remained attached. This snaggle tooth put Ssorog at an early disadvantage. Claws like knives opened wounds in necks, backs, and shoulders. Wenobri's ear was bitten off. Ssorog's nose was sliced open and a bib of blood streamed down his white fur. Bit by bit they took their duel to a wide gravel shoal like an island in the river. It gave firmer footing.

Nikki was not sure either bear would live through the fierce anger of battle. Ultimately, Nikki believed she was responsible. She brought the polar bears and brown bears together. She knew Ssorog was trouble. She should have made Ticcar take him back to Polar Bear Land. If Ssorog triumphs against wise Wenobri, then her dearest hope of saving the polar bears would be ruined. Peace would be shattered. Bears would scatter. And it was too soon: polar bears still knew so little about living off this land, this tundra. Nikki zipped airborne to a space near the combatants. Windy flew along. Followme had no choice: he was going, like it or not. No one paid attention to them.

Courage flooded Nikki, and blood came hot to her face. Her mind slowed down, and she saw each fighting move in slow motion. She needed the agility and sensitivity of bare feet, so she tore off hiking boots and socks. Her hunting knife was sheathed at her waist, and she threw it down with the other castoffs. Her job was peacemaking, not knifing.

It was five minutes into the battle. The bears were tiring and hurting, but still roaring and grappling. Now things happened fast. Nikki determined to stop the battle. Clearly she didn't care if it cost her health or her life. As for Belinda, she had saved Nikki's life once. Now she might have to again.

Nikki thrust her arms overhead and screamed her own battle cry. Gargling screams, piercing screams, a woman warrior's screams. She took a running start, arms pumping, then a hop and a jump. As if springing off a diving board, she launched into the bear fight. With both hands she grabbed Ssorog's tail and twisted it, hard. Then she ran around and did the same to Wenobri. Startled and confused, each shouted and turned away from the fight to see what was happening back there. This gave Nikki her opening. As the bears turned back to wrestle, Nikki scrambled up their stomachs and shoulders to grab an ear of each. Belinda watched and knew those two could not be stopped by that defenseless little human. Charlie-Chum scrambled for the hunting knife. Nikki might be nuts and think she could stop a bear fight with her bare hands, but he wasn't Nikki, and he would defend her at knife point if need be. He took a position crouched at the river's edge, ready to spring into action.

But Nikki beat him to it. In one swift move she swung onto Ssorog's shoulders, riding him, clinging with her hands on his ears and her knees, legs, feet and toes digging in wherever they could, yelling her warrior yells. Now it was Belinda's turn. She tackled Ssorog, cutting his legs out from under him. Ssorog fell on his face and Nikki held on. Belinda sat on his hind end. For good measure, Windy grabbed onto Ssorog's head, wings flapping and claws piercing the bear's hide. Left alone, Wenobri stumbled and fell to the ground, brown fur matted and dark with spilled blood.

CHAPTER SEVENTEEN

ALL HUNG IN THE BALANCE. *Which combatant would lead them? Wenobri or Ssorog?* Polar bears and brown bears crept back to watch their future being determined. Cautiously, Nikki, Belinda, and Windy got off Ssorog. Painfully he rose to his feet, bleeding from many cuts and bites around the face. One eye was gone. One shoulder was wrenched out of its socket, hanging useless by Ssorog's side. Judging by Ssorog's wounds, Wenobri had fought hard and well. But so had Ssorog. Wenobri winced as he got up on all fours. Ssorog had given him several cracked ribs and a chest wound. It was hard to breathe.

And at that moment, before the battle was decided, something extraordinary happened. The gravelly shoal began to quiver. The bears, Nikki, and Charlie-Chum ran to solid ground. Scared, Wenobri and Ssorog hobbled and helped each other along. Quivering gave way to cracking. The ground began to open along jagged seams.

What is this? Nikki wondered in a panic. *An earthquake?* As she watched, river, land, grasses, and shrubs all around them seemed to gather a shared life. They peeled back along the ever-deeper cracks. From far below ground, something huge rose to the surface. It was a living being. Nikki stared in horrified fascination as a giant broke out of the earth. No one was fighting anymore. Bears all around were frozen in place. Nikki and Charlie-Chum clutched each other. Windy was aghast. Followme had nothing to say. They had no thought except to watch the giant.

Nikki imagined it was as tall as the office buildings back home. But she couldn't be sure, because the giant reclined on a lounge that seemed actually to be a whopping big turtle. The turtle was so big that Nikki could only see part of the turtle. Seaweed, water lilies, and fresh streams wove through the giant's hair. Cushions on the turtle's back were mounds of deep, fragrant, fertile soil. From the soil sprang all sorts of plants, especially strawberries, corn, squash, beans, and nut trees. Forests on the turtle's back hid birds, rabbits, deer, bears, and many other animals. All living things actually emerged from the giant's body.

By now Nikki was pretty sure who this was, but she wasn't speaking until spoken to. After all, Nikki might try to stop a bear fight, but she wasn't an idiot. No way was she getting in trouble with a giant.

A live coral snake—gorgeous and poisonous, Nikki knew—curled around the giant's finger like a ring. Half a dozen pumpkin-colored orb spiders draped their delicate wagon-wheel webs over the giant's shoulders. Each spider glowed in the center of her web like a jewel. The giant spoke.

"Do you know who I am?" Her voice was like honey. She didn't sound scary. The giant looked around and finally fixed on Windy. "Certainly you, Windemere Justis Peregrine, know me. Yes?"

Windy was relaxed now. "Yes. You are our mother. Mother Earth. You put earth on Turtle's back. You are the mother of all living things and the earth and waters that sustain them."

"You speak truly, Windemere. The Creator did well to send you here, to aid me. You are a spirit in the form of a falcon. Thank you."

"It is my honor, Mother," Windy said.

"You, polar bear by the name of Ssorog." Mother Earth looked sternly at the mess Ssorog was at the moment, muddy and bloody, one-eyed and limping. She pointed a long arm and finger at him. Squirrels braceleted her wrist, furrily chasing each other's tails around and around. "What were you doing?"

"Uh, what was I doing when, uh ma'am?" Ssorog wasn't in control here, so he had no idea what would be the best answer. He didn't care about a true answer. He just wanted to come out of this on top, where he was before. Darn it, he was just about to knock out Wenobri for good, if this creature hadn't gotten in the way. He did wonder how she knew his name.

"Don't take me for a fool, Son. You were fighting. Who were you tearing apart?"

"I was tearing apart Wenobri, leader of the brown bears, ma'am."

"You may call me Mother."

"Oh, all right," Ssorog muttered under his breath. "Thank you, Mother."

"Now we're getting on. And why, pray tell, were you tearing apart Wenobri?"

"Because he's wise, but I'm powerful. Bears need a powerful leader. Power is my thing, Mother."

"Oh, so you thought it would be all right to kill another bear, just so you could swing your power around? Listen and remember: I did not make bears to kill each other. Especially now that polar bear ice is disappearing. This is a polar bear emergency, I'm sure you know that, since you are a polar bear. Well?"

"Yes, Mother," said Ssorog. He felt like a naughty boy. Which he had been, in fact. "I won't kill other bears."

"Good." Mother Earth deepened her honeyed voice so it sounded like a thousand mother bears crooning to their cubs. Every bear could hear. "Listen and remember, all my bears: There shall be no fighting to death between polar bears and brown bears. Polar bears must live."

Then Mother Earth returned to Ssorog. "And you, Ssorog, listen and remember: Unless power brings life, it is nothing."

"Yes, Mother. I hear you, but I don't understand. I'm strong and smart and I can make other bears do anything I want. That's my power. What should I do with it?"

"You, my powerful polar bear son, shall travel half a moon from here. There gather other polar bears and teach them what you have learned. They need you. You can lead them to life. Be wise as well as powerful."

"Yes, Mother," said Ssorog.

"Now go. You will be always in my care." She reached out and touched each hurt. A new eye grew, his shoulder healed, his cuts were cured, and even his coat became a beautiful, clean white again.

Nikki watched a renewed Ssorog set off. Now he had a life-giving mission, direct from Mother Earth. He had power to save polar bears, and she was sure that's what he would do. Nikki was fascinated by Mother Earth, no longer afraid. *Look at how she had turned big bully so-full-of-himself Ssorog around. Amazing.* Nikki watched a little pink starfish winkle its way down Mother Earth's watery hair. The coral snake, tired of being a ring, slithered off into the woods on turtle's back.

Mother Earth now looked around and found Wenobri, with Belinda beside him, licking his wounds. She called to him. "You, brown bear by the name of Wenobri, come closer. We shall have a little talk. Belinda, you may help him along." Wenobri's eyes were unfocused with pain, and his shallow breathing was too loud, like the sound of a river stumbling over rocks. They hobbled toward Mother Earth and sank to the ground. Belinda let Wenobri lean on her.

"All right, you two. Wenobri. You are the leader here, but it seems you set a very poor example for your bears. What were you doing just now?"

"I was fighting Ssorog, Mother."

"And just why were you doing this?"

"Because he attacked me. I had to fight. It was self-defense."

"Was it? You could have run," Mother Earth said.

"No, I couldn't run, Mother. That would have saved my skin, but it would have left all these brown bears and polar bears to the violent leadership of Ssorog. That bear never has an unselfish thought, and he acts on most of them."

"Yet what if Ssorog won the fight, and you died?"

"Then I would have died trying to stop killing. I would have died to save life. My bears' lives. Mother."

"Please, Mother Earth, don't you see that Wenobri really is dying?" asked Belinda. "You healed that villain Ssorog. Won't you heal my darling Wenobri? He is a gentle bear, and a wise leader."

"Wenobri, my son, listen and remember: A wise leader saves life. In this emergency, polar bears must come in to Brown Bear Land to learn. You have begun well. Your bears have not chased off the newcomers. They have generously shown them where to find food and how to dig, or pluck, or catch it. Your wise leadership made this happen. I commend you, Wenobri."

Then Mother Earth reached out and touched each wounded place. Wenobri's ribs knit together and the tear in his lungs meshed. Wenobri jumped to four feet, sharp-eyed, healed, and full of joy.

"Now go be wise and save life. You will always be in my care."

"Oh, Mother, I, oh, thank, thank you." Wenobri had trouble speaking. Not only because he was overwhelmed by Mother Earth, but also because Belinda was all over him, snuggling and hugging, and he couldn't get a word out. "I will do as you say. It will be my pleasure."

Mother Earth laughed at the two happy bears. To Nikki, her laugh was like rich fruit. *Plums?* The sound made Nikki's heart feel full and purply. Before she hadn't known, but now she did. It was Mother Earth she loved. Everything upon the earth and under the earth and in the waters, all in one body. All as it should be. Every single thing needed and loved. Nikki glimpsed polar bears swaying across tundra on Turtle's back, heading toward the winter ice, all part of Mother Earth. Nikki gazed up at her.

"Now Charlie-Chum, boy human, come closer." Chum let go of Nikki, who he was still holding pretty tightly, and haltingly stepped toward the giant, this good giant who stirred something new inside him. "What were you doing just now?"

"Mother, I was going to save Nikki."

"By getting into the melee with a knife?"

"Yes! She was unarmed and unprotected from the bears' teeth and claws."

"But saving by hurting with a weapon is not your calling, young man. You are called to be a healer. You have made an excellent start, learning from the wise healer at home, and seeking to understand the plants around you here. But there lies a whole expanse of knowledge ahead for you to grasp. And the most important thing is what you possess already: The spirit to heal. This is an *orenda*, a gift from the Creator. This *orenda* will lead you to be a great and powerful healer, and you will help many living beings. You will always be in my care."

"Thank you, Mother. You have made me so happy!" Chum exclaimed, throwing up his hands and feeling a glow flood his spirit.

"Now, you, Nikki Brant, girl human," Mother Earth said. "What were you doing just then?"

"I was trying to stop the fighting, Mama."

"That's clear. But were you out of your mind? You jumped in there completely unprotected, while those battle-crazed bears were going at it with teeth and claws and muscle. Why would an intelligent girl like you do such a foolish thing?"

"I thought I might stop them. Belinda and Windy helped. I had to try. If Wenobri were killed and Ssorog took over, there would be trouble all the time. Polar bears would never learn how to live off the tundra. The only thing left would be starvation, with the ice too far away."

"There's more to it, isn't there, my girl?" said Mother Earth.

At first Nikki felt shy, then she looked Mother Earth straight in the eye, knowing she would understand. "Mama, I did it because I love them. I love the polar bears and that's why I want to save them. I love the brown bears, too, and I love you most of all."

Another purply chuckle came from Mother Earth. Violets now edged her neckline, and her lap was full of plums. Nikki went closer.

"May I come up, Mama?"

"Of course. Don't worry about Turtle. He's very calm and stable. That's why I built the earth upon him."

"Oh," said Nikki and she went closer. She climbed up Turtle's back and up pillows of earth. She came to grasses and grains and tropical plants and arctic plants, all forming Mother Earth's gown. Butterflies and honeybees and gnats and all sorts of bugs were at their business there. Nikki sat in Mother Earth's lap.

"Nikki, the Creator gave you *orendas*, didn't he?" said Mother Earth.

"Yes, Mama. I know how to fly, that's one *orenda*, and Followme brought me the *orenda* of understanding animals and being able to speak to them."

"Indeed," said Mother Earth. "And how do you think you should use these *orendas*?"

"To serve the Creator. And now I know to serve you, Mama."

"And?"

Nikki pondered. "Love. I use the *orendas* to love."

"Well said, my girl. Love is the greatest use of your *orendas*. Now I will use my power to give you a new name. Stand up." And Nikki did so. She was a ragged sight, in a torn and bloody T-shirt and shorts, bare feet, and no knife. She was pretty much just herself and defenseless. Looking down, Nikki saw a path under her feet. It curved ahead and went up and down and disappeared into the forest, then reappeared in the distance.

Nikki returned her gaze to Mother Earth, who brushed Nikki on each shoulder with a glorious branch of flowering crab apple.

Then Nikki heard her say, "I name you Nikki Orenda. By the loving and courageous and intelligent use of your *orendas* to save the polar bears, you have demonstrated a rare quality: You are a soul on the right path. Thus you, yourself, are an *orenda*. An *orenda* possesses tremendous power. The Creator and I expect you to use it for love. Especially for love of Mother Earth." Nikki felt golden inside. She was a soul on the right path.

Mother Earth continued. "That means I expect you to fight for healing of the environment. You and the bears have conducted a brave experiment. But, actually, by learning to live off the tundra, the polar bears have only bought some time. The real solution is that humans must stop global warming, so the sea ice doesn't retreat any further. So polar bears can catch seals the way they are meant to, and remain fat and happy *Ursus maritima*."

"I'm only a kid. Tell me how I can do this," Nikki said.

"Nikki Orenda, you must grab the attention of leaders and of many, many people, and convince them how dire this emergency is. Humans must not waste time to enact their love of the Creator and me, Mother Earth. I will help you show them how and why. Polar bears are the weak link in the chain of life. If polar bears continue to die out, they will be the sign that global warming will be even worse for all of nature and for people around the world."

Nikki understood now how immense the problem is. She felt the weight of responsibility.

"Go back now to your family, and carry on your good work," Mother Earth said.

"But Mama, I want to be with you. I need you. How can I find you again?" asked Nikki.

"Windy can always bring you to me. Don't worry. I love you, Nikki Orenda. You will always be in my care."

Then Windy and Nikki Orenda took flight with Charlie-Chum and Followme, and returned home, full of understanding and the energy to act.

DEAR READER, do you want to help Nikki and the Polar Bears? Go to my website, margaretpollockwrites.com to find out how. See you there! Thank you. MP